# Murder in the Arboretum

By

Leo T. McCall

This book is a work of fiction. Names, characters, places and incidents are the product of the author's imagination. Any resemblance to actual events or locales or persons living or dead is entirely coincidental.

Copyright 2001 by Leo T. McCall

For information regarding this title, please contact:
Leo T. McCall
515 South Lexington Parkway, #106
St. Paul, MN 55116
(651) 699-8458

All rights reserved including the right of reproduction in whole or in part in any form.

Manufactured in the United States of America

ISBN 0-9652038-1-6
Certificate of Registration Library of Congress
March 31, 2001
Mary Beth Peters

Typeset by Stanton Publication Services, Inc.
2402 University Avenue West, Suite 206
St. Paul, MN 55114

Interior design by Rachel Holscher
Cover design by Sarah Purdy

## THE AUTHOR WISHES TO THANK

Ann Keller of Meredith, New Hampshire, for her excellent work in editing this novel

Mary Sweeney, photographer of the rose on the cover of this novel

# Preface

"Far from the madding crowd" of the Twin Cities, the Midwest Arboretum passes serenely through the seasons. A kaleidoscopic of shrubs blaze in the fall until their leaves, withered and sere, dropped into the ravines, ponds, and lakes. In winter, "Ah, bitter chill it was / The owl, for all his feathers, was acold; / The hare limped trembling through the winter grass." Deer steal from the bird feeders and rummage through the carcasses of thousands of species of ornamental plants. With April come cold cloudbursts, but "My heart leaps when I behold a rainbow in the sky." In Minnesota, the question "What is so rare as a day in June?" evokes an answer only those who generally deal with snow six months out of every year can provide. Aromatic lilacs, black-eyed Susans, and whitewater lilies bloom for a transient moment, bloom and spread their aroma for a brief time for the winter weary.

"This," the arboretum's curator is fond of saying, "is a poet's paradise." Until murder among the rose bushes disturbed the landscaper's careful designs, if not nature's.

# Murder in the Arboretum

# Chapter One

Bernard Crow noticed immediately that something was wrong with Ralph Rosenkraatz. Crow had invited the locally famous authority on roses to speak to the new volunteers during a training session at the Midwest Arboretum. With just 140 pounds clinging to his six-foot frame, Rosenkraatz looked as though he were about to melt into a puddle, just like the Wicked Witch of the West. When he was nervous, he fiddled with his belt, which invariably appeared as if it were losing a battle with gravity over control of Rosenkraatz's pants. In his youth, he was an amateur boxer, but not for long. He was pummeled by shorter, huskier opponents who belted him time and again in the stomach until he doubled over just far enough so they could scorch the side of his head. This experience left Rosenkraatz with cauliflower ears ("No, no, cabbage rose ears," he would insist when he was particularly satisfied with himself) and the knowledge that, in a world where only the strong survive, he was sixteen letters on a head stone. After three one-round defeats, he finally took his mother's and brother's advice and quit the fight game. He discovered he was much more suited to the rigors of academia and studied botany at the University of Minnesota.

Crow crossed the lecture room to shake his old friend's hand.

"Rosie," Crow said taking a tray of slides from the taller man, "you look terrible."

"I should, I should," Rosenkraatz said. "Someone is threatening my life, my life, I tell you. Look!"

With that, Rosenkraatz withdrew a slip of paper from his jacket and handed it to Crow.

> Let him that is a true-born gentleman
> And stands upon the honour of his birth,
> If he suppose that I have pleaded truth,
> From off this brier pluck a white rose with me.
> A wax doll of you is burning, Rosie, when it is
>     finished, so are you.

Crow looked puzzled. "Where did you get this?" he asked.

"The mail," Rosenkraatz answered. "It came in the mail."

"Is it some nut's idea of a joke?"

"Yes, yes, I suppose it is," Rosenkraatz replied,

"but should this *nut* make good this threat, bury me in red, I say *red,* roses, ha! ha!"

Crow handed the note back to his friend. "Did you call the police?"

"The police!" Rosenkraatz shot back. "The police? Who has time for them? I'm sure it's just some nut, just as you said, some nut."

Serious or not, Rosencratz could not imagine anyone getting upset enough to post a threat. Despite the fact that he was as big as the movie star Orson Welles and had a voice just like Orson's, deep and sonorous, Rosencratz tried very hard to make sure he offended no one around him and showed the world a wan smile beneath his well-trimmed moustache, now thin and gray just like his hair. He carried a cane with a rose colored handle to move his big body around, but he didn't need it.

Rosenkraatz and Crow hovered over the slide projector, making sure the bulb was not burned out and the remote control worked. The volunteers chatted amongst themselves in small groups, occasionally laughing and shifting their weight from one foot to another.

"Are you ready?" Crow asked.

"Ready?" Rosenkraatz repeated. "Yes, certainly."

Crow walked to the front of the room, hitched up his pants and cleared his throat a few times to get the attention of the volunteers. He motioned them to sit, and then began:

"Mr. Ralph Rosenkraatz needs no introduction for

some of you, but for the rest, I will give you a brief summary of some his exploits."

Although Crow knew the speech by heart, having introduced his friend every year for the past ten years to the volunteer gatherings, he took a card out of his pocket.

"Mr. Rosenkraatz came to the attention of local horticulturists when he was studying botany at the University of Minnesota. He developed a wonderful hybrid which won state-wide and national awards."

Someone coughed in the audience, but when Crow looked up, the spasm had stopped.

"He has served as an advisor to the Lake Harriet Rose Garden right here in the Twin Cities, the White House Rose Garden, and many other rose gardens throughout the United States and the world." Crow paused before finishing with, "I give you one of the world's foremost rose experts, my friend, 'Rosie' Rosenkraatz."

Polite applause followed this paean, which upset Rosenkraatz, who felt he was once more in the ring about to get his ears slapped.

Crow went to dim the lights in the room. Upon the screen shone a slide of a town labeled Marseilles, and Rosenkraatz began.

"My first slides will tell you about the rose in history. No flower has a history as long and meritorious as the rose. The writer Guy de Maupassant called the area between Nice and Marseilles, quote, the land of roses, the birthplace of roses, endquote. Shakespeare mentions the rose over 60 times."

Here Ralph showed a slide of Shakespeare's head.

"I am sure you lovers of roses are acquainted with the War of the Roses. The Earl of Warwick used the white rose as his symbol and the Earl of Suffolk with the red. Does anyone remember the outcome?" Rosenkraatz asked.

It appeared the only one to remember the War of the Roses was the librarian, Bebe Daniels, as she nodded her head and said, "It was a civil war in England fought between the Houses of Lancaster and York. It was named after the supposed badges of the contending parties: the white rose of York and the red of Lancaster."

"Thanks, Bebe," Crow butted in to keep the show going. "Please continue with your slides, Ralph."

"If anyone wants to know more about the 'War of the Roses', just see me at the library," Bebe managed to add.

"We shall begin with roses in history," Rosenkraatz began. "It is reported that, in the Garden of Eden, the white rose blushed and turned red when kissed by Eve."

A stylized Eden with a coy Eve appeared on the screen.

"The first written record I can find of roses occurred in the writings of Homer."

A slide of a Greek warrior flashed on the screen.

"In the *Iliad,*" Rosenkraatz continued, "Homer relates that Achilles' shield was decorated with roses during the siege of Troy in 1205 BC."

A slide of Confucius came next. "Confucius wrote in 551 BC that the Imperial Museum in China had over 500 books on roses.

"In Imperial Roman times, the rose served as a omantic symbol on jewelry, carvings, enamels and ceramics, as well as carpets, stained glass windows, furniture, musical instruments, tapestries, and painted fans used to ward off the heat in the southern climates."

A slide with men and women wearing togas accompanied the information about Rome.

"Late in the 18th century the rose appeared on candlesticks, vases and bottles," Rosenkraatz said as he pushed the forward button and up popped a picture of some rose designs on vase.

"In Deadwood, South Dakota, the House of Roses sits on a lot hacked into the cliff's surrounding the city," Rosenkraatz said as a slide of Wild Bill Hickock appeared on the screen. "It was built in 1876, the same year James Bulter Hickock, better known as Wild Bill, was shot playing cards in Saloon Number 10. The twenty-seven room Queen Anne mansion was owned by James Wilson, whose wife Victoria imported rose bushes from England, thus giving the house its name."

Rosenkraatz switched slides to show the Deadwood

home. "The roses at the house come from those English roses and are now 125 years old.

"In another rough and tumble American town," Rosenkraatz continued, "is another famous rose. The world's largest rose tree grows in Tombstone, Arizona," Rosenkraatz went on. "It was planted in 1885 and is an amazing example of R. Pankslea. It has spread to over 8,000 square feet of patio and it is still growing."

A couple people in the audience murmured as a slide of the Tombstone rose tree replaced the House of Roses in Deadwood.

"You all have heard Dorothy Parker's comment, 'a rose is a rose is a rose'? That is not true . . . and I'll tell you why."

Bebe Daniels broke in. "Actually Gertrude Stein wrote that in *Sacred Emily*."

"What?" asked Rosenkraatz.

"Gertrude Stein wrote 'a rose is a rose is a rose,'" Bebe repeated, "not Dorothy Parker. Parker wrote 'Why is it no one every sent me yet / One perfect limousine, do you suppose? / Ah no, it's always just my luck to get / One perfect rose.'"

Several in the audience laughed out loud as Rosenkraatz blushed. A hum could be heard above snickering.

"Everything's comin' up roses, right Mr. Rosenkraatz?" asked a member of the audience in reference to the tune that was being hummed.

The comment made Rosenkraatz blush an even darker shade of red, but he managed to blurt out, "Ah, yes, the rose in song. Do you know any others?"

Wendall Holmes stood up and blurted out a few bars of "The Yellow Rose of Texas."

"Do you know how it came about?" Ralph asked.

Holmes answered, "'The Yellow Rose of Texas' was written for Emily Morgan, who helped the Texans win their freedom from Mexico. Songs about roses are a specialty of mine."

Holmes began to hum "The Rose of Tralee."

"And how did that song come about?" asked Ralph.

"The original Rose was a hat shop assistant, Mary O'Sullivan, with whom William Mulchinock, the writer of the song, fell hopelessly in love."

"Any other rose songs?" asked Ralph.

"As Jimmy Durante use to say, 'I got a million of em,'" the smiling Holmes replied and started to sing: "Sweetest 'lil' feller / Everybody knows / Dunno what ter call him / But he's mighty like a rose."

Some of the volunteers clapped when he finished in a high tenor.

"I could, if you liked, sing 'Moonlight and Roses,' 'Rose Marie,' 'Mexicali Rose,' 'Abe's Irish Rose,' 'Second Hand Rose,' 'The Rose in Her Hair,' 'Only a Rose,' 'My Wild Irish Rose,' 'Rose Room,' 'The Rose of San Antonio,' 'The Last Rose of Summer,' 'Mighty Like a Rose,' 'Sweet Rose O'Grade,' 'The Roses of

Picardy,' and my favorite, 'Ramblin' Rose,' but of course, I can hum and any other song containing the word 'rose' in its title," Holmes ended with a flourish and sat.

A volunteer raised her hand. Rosenkraatz pointed to her and said, "Since you are all new to me, could you introduce yourselves before you ask your questions?"

"My name is Virginia Haynes. Frankly, I am not crazy about roses, but my boss is, and that is why I am here, to find out which roses grow best in the cold, Minnesota climate."

Once a brunette, Virginia streaked her hair with gray over brown.

As secretary to multi-millionaire Ernest Erickson, she was responsible for keeping fresh roses in his hotels. Her secretary's desk contained two letter holders—incoming and outgoing—neither of which was full more than five minutes at any time during the day.

Her introduction of herself to Rosenkraatz was honest, for other secretaries near her desk often heard her mumble "Those damn roses," whenever Erickson asked her about the flowers.

She was feared by all employees for what she could tell the boss about who was working hard and who wasn't. Furthermore, she was not very likable. She never exchanged gossip at the water cooler, didn't share problems in the break room, rarely said hello unless forced to, and hardly ever smiled, except when she came into contact with Erickson's driver. High-heeled shoes clicking down the corridor warned everyone, "Here comes Virginia."

Rosenkraatz visibly relaxed. No one dared dispute his knowledge of shrub roses and Old Garden roses and why they survived the Minnesota cold.

"Shrub roses and Old Garden roses are popular across the northern tier of the United States," Rosenkraatz said, "as gardeners realize that these plants provide excellent floral quality in combination with disease tolerance and winter hardiness. With these roses, you can minimize pesticides and delineate the labor-intensive job of protecting them from low winter temperatures.

"The Old Garden roses are noted for their fragrance. They are less demanding of soil conditions and have higher levels of disease resistance and winter hardiness.

"Shrub roses will also re-bloom during the growing season. More often than not, shrub roses are larger and more branched than Hybrid Teas and Fire bushes."

"I have a question," Virginia interrupted. "What is the difference between Old Garden roses and shrub roses?"

"An Old Garden rose is normally pink or mauve or maroon or purple and crimson and built like a beautiful movie star—Lauren Bacall, while a shrub rose is more like the former President's wife, Barbara Bush.

So, when you think of a Shrub rose, think of Mrs. Bush."

"Why is it like Mrs. Bush?" asked Virginia.

"The plant is more short and squat," answered Rosenkraatz as someone else raised a hand in the audience. "I forgot to thank you for your delightful treatise regarding songs about roses, but I don't think I caught your name."

"Wendall Holmes—no relation to Sherlock," Wendall said. He always added "no relation to Sherlock" when he introduced himself.

Rosenkraatz noticed that Holmes wore a white rose in his lapel. What he didn't know was that Holmes always wore a white rose in his lapel.

Holmes was an impeccable dresser; shoes shined morning, noon and night; pants pressed razor sharp; button down shirt, and tie, always matching the color of his suit.

Holmes's asked, "What is the deadliest disease for a rose?"

"Black spot," Rosenkraatz said. "This can be detected—no pun intended, Mr. Holmes—when small circular black spots develop on upper surfaces."

"How does the disease of black spot develop, and how is it spread?" asked Holmes.

Rosenkraatz replied, "The disease is caused by several fungi."

As Sherlock Holmes, his namesake, might do, Holmes came back with, "Can you name the fungi?"

"All I can tell you are the symptoms. The leaf surrounding these spots turns yellow and this chlorosis spreads until the leaflet is dropped from the plant."

"For some newcomers here who might not know, what does fungi mean?" Holmes pressed.

Rosenkraatz hitched up his pants. "A fungus is a single-celled multi-nucleus organism that lives by decomposing the organic material in which it grows. Examples are mushrooms, rusts, molds, and yeasts."

"I guess that is why some of my so-called friends call me Mr. Fungus," interjected Crow.

Rosenkraatz kept reciting, "Black spot is called Diplocarpon. Any other questions, Mr. Holmes?"

"Just one," replied Holmes. "Would you mind spelling Diplocarpon?"

"Not at all," said Ralph. Loudly he spelled, "D-I-P-L-O-C-A-R-P-O-N."

While Crow was spelling Diplocarpon, Holmes took a slip of paper out of his pocket to write down the spelling. As he took the paper another slip of paper fell on the floor. Rita Rosetta, another of the volunteers, picked it up. She couldn't help herself from reading a prescription on it that read, "Zyprexa" before handing it to Holmes.

"Thank you," said Holmes as Rita gave him the prescription.

Rita Rosetta then raised her hand.

"My name is Rita Rosetta, and I own a floral shop. Can a rose bush get black spot overnight?"

After leaving the nunnery, Rita had gone back to school and had become a nurse's aide. She had worked for a short time in a hospital. Depressed working around dying cancer patients, she found a position in a flower shop. With her father's money behind her, she soon owned her own floral business.

She liked the pleasant surroundings of a flower shop. She found serenity in arranging flowers for weddings and anniversaries and birthdays. She hired an assistant to attend to funerals. Neighborhood customers called her Miss 5 x 5, five feet tall and five feet wide. She always wore soft leather shoes . . . she didn't want to disturb her roses. She frowned on customers who came in slamming her front door and banging her bell for attention. Her straight black hair had not a curl in sight. The customers who talked about Miss 5 x 5 behind her back often said, "Nothing beautiful about Rita but her name."

Rosenkraatz had momentarily lost his concentration and had to ask Rita to repeat what she had asked.

"My question, Mr. Rosenkraatz, is this: can a rose bush get black spot overnight?"

"No," answered Ralph. "A fungi grows insidiously, like cancer."

At this, Rita blanched, but Ralph kept on.

"It does not come overnight like sudden fear," Rosenkraatz finished.

"Thank you," said a very disturbed Rita.

Rosenkraatz noticed that Virginia was seated very

close to a good-looking man and directed his next statement to him.

"Have you any questions?" he asked John Jones.

"Yes, I do," replied Jones as he bashfully withdrew his hand from Virginia's.

Jones was chauffeur to Ernest Erickson, the multi-millionaire hotel magnate. He was handsome and stood six feet tall. His black curly hair and brown eyes appealed to most women over thirty and, in this case, completely enthralled Virginia. When not in uniform, he dressed nattily: two toned shoes, gabardine slacks and polo shirts.

"My name is John Jones. I am Mr. Erickson's chauffeur. Personally, I don't care for roses. Frankly, I prefer mums. But I was wondering, why are roses considered the symbol of love?"

Before Rosenkraatz could offer an answer, Crow interjected, "If you don't like roses, Mr. Jones, why did you come here today?"

"I take my boss wherever he wants to go," replied Jones.

"And who is your boss again?"

"I am his employer," said Ernest Erickson rising.

"And you, sir?"

"My name is Ernest Erickson. I own several local hotels and a few others around the world. This man, Jones, is my chauffeur."

Erickson was a hotel magnate. His reason for being at this particular seminar was an obvious one. Every hotel of his had a suite called "The Rose Room," where any guest booking in advance would find a dozen roses in his or her room upon entering. So Erickson kept track, through his secretary, of all new species of roses which had new colors or fragrances. He decided to become a volunteer at the Arboretum to keep up-to-date on "What's new." His build was similar to Rita Rosetta's . . . short and plump, 5 x 5. He smoked expensive imported Bering Casinos cigars and wore tailor-made suits—always either gray or blue with ties to match.

Unknown to all but his chauffeur, he carried a pearl-handled revolver because he lived with a constant fear of being kidnapped.

Crow continued his address to Erickson, "We here at the Arboretum are familiar with your continued support of our rose gardens. It is an honor to finally meet you in person. Your idea of furnishing one room in each of your worldwide hotels with a dozen roses is ingenious. What a pleasant surprise to enter a hotel room and find a dozen roses waiting."

Ralph cleared his throat. "In answer to your question: over the centuries the rose has inspired poets, painters, and writers, like myself, so there is one conclusion; the rose stands alone in beauty and has power to intrigue more than any other flower. I can't prove it, but I am sure Adam sent Eve a rose when they gamboled in the Garden of Eden. You are a romantic if you are born in the month of the roses—June."

"I don't know why roses are the symbol of love," Erickson said, "but I know they sure as hell work. I wooed my own wife with roses, a dozen per day until she said yes."

"Any particular rose?" Crow asked.

"The most popular color of course . . . red, for passion."

Crow responded, "Red is the most popular, or course. Can you give me more detail on the red, how fragrant, how tall, what shade of red and then what cluster?"

Erickson's quick reply startled Crow. "Two feet tall, blood red, the fragrance of Channel #5. From now on, though, I don't want to have to dig them in the fall and replant in the spring."

Crow smiled. "You should build your own greenhouses."

Erickson turned to his secretary, Virginia.

"Do we have the time or, I mean, do you have the time to run a greenhouse along with your job?"

"Not this year, Mr. Erickson. I am too busy," a very concerned Virginia stammered.

Crow tried to get the presentation back on track. "Do you have any favorites, Rosie?"

"The best color for fragrance, in my opinion," said Rosenkraatz, "is lavender. Lavender roses bloom all year long."

Bebe Daniels raised her hand. Before Rosenkraatz recognized her, she blurted out, "My name is Bebe

Daniels. My father's name was Daniels. So when I was born, he named me after his favorite actress of the time, Bebe Daniels, over my mother's objection I assure you."

Everyone in the room offered a pained smile, hoping Bebe would get to her point. What they didn't know was that Bebe liked to talk. As a librarian, she had to be quiet most of her life, so she took every opportunity outside the library to display her knowledge. She talked so much when not at work that her brother once offered, "I'll pay someone to listen to you."

"I was wondering, Mr. Crow, if you have a favorite rose?" Bebe asked.

"Actually, Ms. Bebe, you remind me of my favorite shrub bush—Angel Face," Crow gushed. "The urn shaped ruby buds open slowly to double ruffle blossoms of rich lavender, extremely fragrant."

"Thank you," said Bebe obviously pleased with the answer.

Ernest Erickson barged in with something that bothered him. "Mr. Rosenkraatz, are you a botanist or a horticulturist?"

"I am a horticulturist by vocation and a botanist with a U of M degree," Rosenkraatz answered.

"Let's all give Mr. Rosenkraatz a hand," shouted Holmes.

Caught up in the moment, everyone gave a polite clap for Rosenkraatz without quite knowing why.

This was too much tomfoolery for no-nonsense

Virginia. She objected, "I have come to this meeting about roses to find out how to grow them and keep them alive here in the cold, cold north. I have a suggestion on how this meeting should be handled: Ask each person here what he grows best in Minnesota."

Crow said, "Good idea, Virginia. To start off, why don't you name yours."

Cleverly, Crow had tossed the ball back into Virginia's court. Virginia didn't hesitate, "My favorite is a salmon Old Garden rose."

Rosenkraatz said, "As you know, the first rose was red, and to get salmon we have to go to hybrids."

Erickson asked, "What am I to learn about roses that will help me to decide what roses I should pick for my hotel?"

"We are never too old to learn, Mr. Erickson," smiled Crow, meaning no disrespect for Erickson's age, although he obviously was the oldest volunteer.

Bebe Daniels didn't like the attention taken away from her. She was not an actress like her namesake, but she did like attention. "I have a list of the questions most asked in the library about roses. Mr. Crow, can you tell me," she said, taking the list from her handbag, "would it be okay to use a Swiss Army knife to prune my roses?"

Crow answered, "The best type of shears are the anvil-type pruning sheers. The Swiss Army knife is okay if it is clean and sharp."

"Next question," Bebe continued. "When is the best time to plant roses?"

Rosenkraatz interrupted impatiently, "When they become available at your nearest local nursery."

Unfazed, Bebe droned on. "What are the most popular roses in the world?"

An easy question for Crow, who almost shouted out, "The hybrid teas!"

"What color?"

"Big Ben and Kentucky Derby."

Crow gave his all on the answer, "Big Ben, Kentucky Derby, Dolly Parton, Mr. Lincoln, Oklahoma, and my favorite of all the Hybrid Tea Roses—Sweet Surrender."

"I don't think you are answering my question," insisted Virginia. "What category of roses is best here in the North?"

"No problem," said Crow. "Shrub roses and Old Garden roses."

"What Shrub Roses and Old Garden Roses should they get from their nursery?" demanded Virginia.

"It is most fortunate that you bring up this subject right now," Rosenkraatz cut in. "I have a manual coming out next month on the effects of snow cover. The rose for the North and how to make it last right up to -20 degrees below. And I will list the roses that you don't have to bury for the winter—the ones that will show up just like the Twins in the spring."

The always-practical Erickson asked, "What will your manual cost us?"

"I don't know yet; my printer will tell me soon."

For the first time, L.T. Bush, who had just entered the room a few minutes earlier, raised his hand.

Crow acknowledged him, "Your name, sir?"

"L.T. Bush is my name and getting back to your question about what is your favorite rose—my favorite rose is the Florabunda Nearly Wild. I like it when it comes out pink and emits a heavenly fragrance."

L.T. Bush was well known at the Arboretum because of the notoriety gained by his best-selling book *The Rose in Her Hair*.

His suit, the opposite of Erickson's, was, in capital letters, SLOPPY. He wore purple shirts and yellow ties, and unpressed khaki pants. His salt and pepper hair, heavy on the sodium chloride, covered his ears. White walking shoes were his trademark. In his younger days, Bush was a baseball pitcher for local municipal teams. He had three pitches—slow, slower and really slow. He was so slow his catcher often caught the pitches barehanded. No need for a catcher's mitt with L.T. on the mound. He had the bad habit of peering at anyone and everyone through the bottom part of his bifocal lens . . . as if he didn't think them worthy of talking to him.

Bush was never on time for anything; he gained attention by strolling in for appointments usually 30 minutes late. He liked to work in dirt and that is why he became a volunteer at the Arboretum.

"You sure know your roses," said Crow after L.T. Bush mentioned the Florabunda Nearly Wild."

The novel *The Rose In Her Hair* was not a masterpiece on the love and care of roses, but a murder story written by L.T. Bush for the Sherlock Holmes Literary Society, of which he was a member.

After its publication, he was in trouble with fellow members of the Sherlock Holmes Society.

L.T. Bush's strategy was a simple one. In his novel he murdered a member of the Society he didn't like and challenged other members to find the guilty one. The real members didn't like being a part of his poorly written novel.

After this exchange between Bush and Crow, John Jones and Virginia Haynes stood up, excused themselves and tried to depart the room hand in hand.

Crow blocked their exit at the door.

"Rosenkraatz isn't over with the slides just yet."

"I want to show Virginia the garden of roses I promised to give her," said Jones.

Crow was not happy about the attitude of these two.

"What is Rosenkraatz going to show us next, roses in cooking?" asked the sassy Virginia.

Crow said, "I wouldn't be surprised. And he told me that he really is going to show something interesting for the ladies, the Perfumed Rose."

Jones and Virginia did not heed Crow at all and left the room.

Crow returned to his seat and told Rosenkraatz, "Those two don't know what they are missing."

"I'll tell you what they are missing." Rosenkraatz spoke loudly for all to hear. "I am going to show all you women just how to make the perfumed rose. This method was used 2,000 years ago.

His slide depicted a dancing girl costumed in Roman garb.

"It's a very simple formula. Just steep fragrant rose petals in boiling water. The Princess Jahan, wife of the Mogul Emperor was said to have asked for the oil floating on the surface of her rose bath to be skimmed off. When this was done, it was found to be highly fragrant."

As his last word on perfumed roses, Ralph said with a flourish, "True attar of roses is such a concentrated perfume that it takes 10,000 roses of suitable fragrance to produce one third fluid ounce."

"True attar is the product of the very rich," added Erickson to whom this observation was of interest.

Rosenkraatz nodded in the direction of Erickson, who seemed unconcerned that his secretary and driver had left the meeting.

"As soon as I finish discussing the rose in history," said Rosenkraatz, "I'd like to talk about roses in cooking, herbal roses, rose gardens, and rose troubles."

Bebe Daniels couldn't stay silent any longer.

"What about movie names concerning roses?" she asked. "My father kept a list of movies made with a rose mentioned in the title: *The Rose, The Rose and the Sword, Rosemarie, Rose of the Cimarron, Rose of the Ranco, The Rose of Washington Square,*

*The Rose Tatoo, Rosebud, Roseanne McCoy, The Purple Rose of Cairo . . ."*

The meeting was getting out of hand and so Crow stepped in.

"I think Ralph would like to continue," he said as politely as he could to Bebe, who bowed slightly toward him and sat down.

"The rose is praised all over the world," said Ralph as a slide of the globe appeared on the screen. "The rose is well known all over the Northern Hemisphere. In English, French, and Norwegian, a rose is named 'rose.' In Italian, Polish, Spanish, Portuguese and Latin it's 'rosa.' In Dutch it is 'roost.' In Bohemian it is 'ricza.' In German it is 'rosen' and Greek it is 'rhoden.' But a rose by any name would smell as sweet."

With this last remark, Bush left the room.

"The first best seller in books was *The Romance of the Rose,* a 13th century allegory in French, written in long hand, no doubt. The Taj Mahal's pool was strewn at night with rose petals and skimmed off before Muntez Mahal bathed."

"The Empress Josephine of France had beautiful and lovely eyes but lousy teeth; and when she smiled, she covered her mouth with a bouquet of roses."

Then L.T. Bush came back to the room.

"The poet Burns wrote," continued Rosenkraatz as he pushed a button to send in a slide the Scottish poet, "'O my Luve's like a red red rose/ That's newly sprung in June.'"

"In the age of chivalry, now long gone, I assure you, the petals of the rose embroidered on the sleeves of knights were highly symbolic as the knights went forth to 'deeds of derring-do.'" On the screen came a slide of an armored knight with a rose on his shield.

"The interest in roses grows everywhere. Today there are 17,000 members in the American Rose Society."

L.T. Bush interrupted Rosenkraatz with a question. "Where are you getting all this information on roses?"

"Mr. Bush, I didn't make this up. All of this information on roses came right from books in Bebe Daniels' library," responded Ralph.

Then came a knock at the door.

"Here are the box lunches you ordered," said a voice as someone handed Crow the nine boxes.

"Are they just the way I ordered them?" asked Crow.

The voice behind the door said, "You bet. Five roast beef, three cheese and one peanut butter."

Crow fumbled through his billfold and handed money to the outstretched hand.

"Go ahead, Ralph, don't let this visit stop you," Crow said, then smiled at Bebe. "Ms. Daniels, will you mark each box with the list I gave you so each volunteer gets the sandwich he or she asked for earlier. Will you? Thanks for the nod."

"You're welcome," Bebe said.

Rosenkraatz continued, "Before I proceed with my

slides, let us pause and take questions you might have."

L.T. Bush broke in with a question.

"When is the best time to plant here in Minnesota bare root roses? And also, when is the best time to plant potted roses?"

Ralph answered, "Bare root roses, April 10 to May 20; potted roses, May 1 to July 31."

"How do you know that is the best time?"

Crow spoke up. "It's in his book *Roses I Have Known*."

"Have you read it?" L.T. Bush kept on.

"Yes," said Crow.

"Then could you tell me what are the major classes of roses?" Bush asked.

"The classes of roses are Floribunda, Grandiflora, climber and rambler, miniature, Alba, Centifolia, shrub and wild," Crow offered.

L.T. Bush couldn't help himself from saying, "The Hybrid Teas are the most widely grown roses all over the world. You missed them."

"You're right," Crow said, "I guess I'll have to eat crow. Ha. Ha. Ha."

"In my book, *The Rose in Her Hair*," Bush said with an emphasis on the word *my*, "I noted that Teas grow long stems, come in bright colors, and bear more roses of all the varieties. And I will tell you something else . . . they bloom profusely throughout the growing season."

Just then into the room came John Jones and Virginia, all out of breath. John spoke first.

"Someone has poisoned the roses!"

Bernard Crow set down his coffee and jumped to his feet.

"What roses have been poisoned?"

"Those in the garden," cried Virginia.

"Close the gates. Let no one out of the grounds!" cried L.T. Bush to no one in particular. He prided himself on always being the first to move into action.

"Is there only one way out of here?" Erickson wanted to know.

Crow filled him in. "There is only one road out of here. On foot, however, there are acres on which to escape."

"How could anyone kill the beautiful roses?" the emotional Rita Rosetta sobbed.

"Very easily," offered the all-knowing L.T. Bush. "Any hardware store sells all kinds of weed killer to do the job. To name just a few, how about Dragon, the poison ivy and poison weed killer, or Roundup, the sure shot killer of weeds and ivy? It also kills the root."

"Why do you know so much about killers for weeds and ivy?" asked Erickson.

"In the mystery story business you have to know all the killers," said a smug L.T. Bush. "In any event, I recommend that someone call the police."

"I was just on my way to do that," said Crow.

Wendall Holmes finally spoke up and suggested they all eat since nothing could be done until the police arrived.

Rosenkraatz agreed with Holmes that there was not reason to waste a good box lunch. He turned off the slide projector and put his notes back in order, relieved to have a reason to stop sharing his wisdom with what seemed to be for the most part an uncaring and ungrateful audience.

Crow returned from his office. "An officer should be here within an hour," he announced. "Bebe, are the boxes all marked and is the coffee ready?"

"Yes," Bebe said from the dining room.

Crow whispered in Rosenkraatz's ear, "I got you a peanut butter sandwich for lunch, O.K.?"

Rosenkraatz whispered back, "Wonderful."

Bebe appeared and said, "Lunch shall now be served. The box lunches are marked, just as Mr. Crow requested."

All the volunteers followed her into the dining room.

Bebe handed each one a box as they came to her. She said, "Crow, here is your beef; Virginia, here is your beef; Wendall Holmes, your beef; Rita, your cheese; Mr. Erickson, your beef; L.T. Bush, sorry no ham, just beef; and last, but not least, Ralph Rosenkraatz, peanut butter."

"Thank you, Bebe," said Crow. "In the cooler you will find bottles of Coca-Cola and Seven-Up. There are glasses on the counter and ice in that container," he said pointing. "If anyone needs anything else, just let me know."

Several people got up to help themselves and others to the soft drinks.

For the first time, everyone was silent as each volunteer, Crow and Rosenkraatz began to devour their sandwiches.

Suddenly, Rosenkraatz stood up and started to choke.

"Can you talk, Ralph?" an alarmed Crow asked.

L.T. Bush grabbed Rosenkraatz from the back and tried to force Ralph to breathe. It didn't work.

Rosenkraatz fell over the table to the floor, still choking.

Then he lay still.

Crow lurched toward him, tripping over the table in his excitement. By that time, Bush had felt his wrist for a pulse and found none.

L.T. put his ear to Rosenkraatz's chest, stood up and said, "He is dead."

Virginia cried, "How can you be sure? We should call an ambulance."

Regaining his balance, Crow went back to his office phone and dialed 911.

During the commotion, Holmes lit a cigarette. Bebe scolded him for being inconsiderate. Holmes looked for someplace to snuff it out. Finding none, he gently worked it between his thumb and index finger to put it out.

LT. Bush fanned Rosenkraatz's face with his notebook, as if it was the least he could do for the corpse.

The paramedics arrived within fifteen minutes. Looking like some kind of space crew—all Velcro and business-like, they dropped their cases and placed a mask on Ralph's face. After an appropriate amount of time fussing over the deceased, they placed the lifeless form on a gurney and packed oxygen tanks, monitors, tubes and wires around his torso as if this technological ice could revive the victim.

As the paramedics carried the body out, an envelope fell from Rosenkraatz's hand.

One of the paramedics picked up the envelope, read it quickly, then asked, "Who is Bernie Crow?"

Crow stepped up at once and said: "I am. Why?"

The paramedic handed the envelope to Crow and hurried away.

Crow went to a corner of the room and read the letter:

Dear Bernie:

Don't be alarmed at what I am to tell you. But one of your volunteers is threatening my life!!! I don't know who wrote it, for it has no signature. This crackpot (or whoever it is) is burning a wax model of me. It sounds like voodoo or a hex of some kind. This letter writer says that this wax model of me will burn out in two days, intimating that is how long I have to live. The postscript on letter reads: "When this wax is all melted, you will be done, too." Should this nut make good his or her threat, bury me in red roses . . . HA HA.

                              Ralph Rosenkraatz

Along with the note was a poem.

### Sister Helen

"Why did you melt your waxen man,
Sister Helen?
Today is the third since you began."
"The time was long, yet the time ran,
Little brother."
(O Mother, Mary Mother,
Three days today, between Hell and Heaven!)

"O Sister Helen, you heard the bell,
Sister Helen!
More loud than the vesper-chime it fell."
"No vesper-chime, but a dying knell,
Little brother!"
(O Mother, Mary Mother,
His dying knell, between Hell and Heaven!)

"Oh the wind is sad in the iron chill,
Sister Helen,

And weary sad they look by the hill."
"But he and I are sadder still,
Little brother!"
(O Mother, Mary Mother,
Most sad of all, between Hell and Heaven!)

"See, see, the wax has dropped from its place,
Sister Helen,
And the flames are winning up apace!"
"Yet here they burn but for a space,
Little brother!"
(O Mother, Mary Mother,
Here for a space, between Hell and Heaven!)

L.T. Bush overheard Crow talking to the paramedics and asked Crow, "What is this all about . . . ?"

Crow turned to L.T. "I think that my friend Ralph may have been poisoned; it was more than just a heart attack."

"Why . . . he had all the symptoms of a heart attack that I know of."

"Here, nosey. Read this letter yourself and tell me your thoughts," said Crow as he handed over the letter.

L.T. read the letter and gave it back to Crow. "Obviously we need to show this to the police and have someone perform an thorough autopsy."

Bernard Crow took the letter to the phone and made his second call to the police that day.

The next day the following obituary appeared in the morning papers.

### ROSENKRAATZ

Ralph "Rosie" Rosenkraatz, age 45, of Roseville, died of heart failure yesterday as he was showing his personal slide collection about roses. Master's Degree from the U of M in horticulture, minor in botany. Former president of the American Rose Society—Twin Cities Division. Also a member of the American Association of Botanical Gardens and staff member of the American Rhododendron Society and past member of the American Primrose Society. Survivors include his wife, Lauren. Funeral services at Fort Snelling Burial Grounds, Tuesday June 10th. Memorials to charity of choice.

The following day a different headline appeared.

"Foul play suspected in death of rose author Ralph Rosenkraatz"

The rose world mourns today the loss of one of its own—Ralph Rosenkraatz. He dropped dead on Tuesday while lecturing at the Arboretum. A call to local police lead to an autopsy which revealed he had been poisoned. Police are withholding details pending an investigation.

His passing will be felt by thousands of friends of roses. His book *Roses I Have Known* made the New York Times best-seller list for many months after its publication. Each year he would depart from his home here in Roseville, Minnesota, and travel the world showing his slides and sharing all his knowledge of the history and romance of roses. His favorite hobby was giving Merit Badges to young Boy Scouts seeking merit badges in botany.

On the morning the newspaper article reported Rosenkraatz's murder, E.E. Erickson phoned Bernard Crow.

"Hello, Crow, this is Erickson. Are you busy?"

"For you, I am always available," said Crow.

"Good," Erickson said. "I am worried about all this bad publicity concerning the Arboretum and murder."

"I'll tell you something about heart attacks and other signs of death. Arsenic also can cause the same symptoms as a heart attack," said Erickson.

"You might have deduced from the newspaper that the autopsy revealed that he did die from poison, yet they don't know if it was arsenic," said a very worried Crow.

"What did Rosenkraatz eat that was different from the rest of us?"

Crow blurted out, "He was the only one to have a peanut butter sandwich."

"And where did that come from?" demanded Erickson.

"It came from your catering service," Crow replied.

"For God's sake, Crow, don't ever mention my name or my service, whatever you do!" Erickson exclaimed.

"You have nothing to do with the investigations. But let us wait and see what the police uncover. I assume that we all will be called in on the investigation," continued Crow.

"This may seem harsh to you, Crow, but I am more concerned about my rose bushes out in the Arboretum field than who did away with your friend Rosenkraatz," said Erickson.

"That *is* rather harsh," admitted Crow.

"The police have a problem here. Who would want to kill a man who devoted his life to roses?" asked Erickson.

"Nobody I can think of among my volunteers," replied Crow.

"My last words to you, Crow," threatened Erickson, "are: if you want me to keep donating to the Arboretum, you will keep my name out of all of this!"

# Chapter Two

The day after the death of Rosenkraatz, the city police put Michael Moore on the case. Captain Moore was no ordinary police officer. He was a former FBI employee who specialized in fingerprint analysis. His primary asset to the police department was the dyspeptic look he gave all suspects, making them feel guilty even if they were innocent. He knew nothing about roses, but he could tell you who batted before and after Babe Ruth on the New York Yankees team of 1927. So he called in one of the police department's consultants, his daughter Madeline Moore.

Madeline Moore was a mathematician and amateur botanist but was better known for her detective skills. Often the police employed her to assist in murder cases because she had an uncanny ability to ferret out the criminal. This, plus she had an "in" in the police department—her father was Michael Moore. Michael knew she knew her roses, having roses in her own back yard. She was a member of the volunteer group at the Arboretum.

Moore told her, "Madeline, I need you on this one—a double murder case. A man has been killed at the Arboretum and someone killed some roses."

"I sometimes think that never blows so red/ The Rose as where some buried Caesar bled," quoted Madeline from Edward Fitzgerald.

Moore said, "You got that right. In any case, you know your way around the Arboretum. Why don't you come out to the Arboretum with me to snoop around?

"Do you mean to say after Rosenkraatz died you let the volunteers all go home?" Captain Moore asked Bernard Crow in his office after arriving with his daughter.

"What was I supposed to do?" returned Crow.

"I assume you have a list of their names and addresses," said Captain Moore.

"Of course. I'll have my secretary get you a copy." Crow picked up the phone, said a few words into the receiver, then gave his attention back to the two detectives. "The list will be here shortly."

Madeline asked, "Where were you when the murder occurred?"

Crow tried to sound nonplussed. "Who said there was a murder?"

"The report came to us from the Coroner's office. That is why Miss Moore and I are here," said Captain Moore.

"In this case, trying to make a case for death by natural causes just didn't add up," said Miss Moore, affectionately called by her associates the Mad Mathematician.

"When two plus two make five . . . I call for Madeline," said Captain.

"Tell us all you know and just what happened the day of the murder," Moore asked.

So Bernard began.

"Each year I invite a guest speaker to address my new volunteers here at the Arboretum. This year it was Mr. Ralph Rosenkraatz, well known world wide by friends of flowers and roses."

"Did anybody besides you know Mr. Rosenkraatz was going to be speaking here that day?" inquired Madeline.

"Not to my knowledge," said Mr. Crow. "Why do you want to know that?"

Michael Moore said, "Most murders are not committed by strangers."

This father-daughter detective combination had begun to rile Crow.

It didn't help his disposition when Madeline asked, "Did you have any reason to dislike Rosenkraatz— perhaps professional jealousy?"

"Certainly not. I would consider him one of my closest friends," said Crow.

"How and when did you first meet Rosenkraatz?" asked Moore.

"I met Rosenkraatz on the day he married my sister."

The always-practical Madeline quipped, "Did it last?"

"What?" asked a truly puzzled Crow.

"The marriage," answered Captain Moore.

"Not very long," Crow said. "My sister ran away from home to go on a tour of rose gardens with this guy, Rosenkraatz. He never married her while they were on the tour. She never wrote home of this escapade."

"What did your mother think of that?" asked Michael.

"She didn't approve, of course. Then one bright June morning last year, in came my sister and Rosenkraatz with the news they were getting married that day. My sister openly confessed her mistake and told me she had no hold on this rose lover until she threatened to leave him and go back home. So he said 'Let's go home and get married.' That's how I met Rosie."

"How romantic," said Madeline.

"So now you hire him to lecture on roses?" asked Michael.

"I hire him because he knows roses. I admit I was not happy with him for treating my sister like a second-hand Rose. I was embarrassed because all my friends knew that my sister had run away with this man. But I got over it and came to admire him. Even after my sister and he divorced, we continued to be friends. If you're implying that…"

"We're not implying anything," said Captain Moore. "We have been told that Mr. Rosenkraatz had traces of a foreign element in his blood that probably killed him."

Mr. Crow defensively said, "All I can tell you is we had a break in his slide show, and we each had a sandwich and a soft drink."

"Did Mr. Rosenkraatz have anything other than what the rest of you ate?" asked Madeline.

"We all had sandwiches ordered to be delivered at the break. I believe Ralph had a peanut butter sandwich."

"Who delivered the sandwiches?" asked Madeline.

"They were brought to us from a downtown business. I got them from a delivery boy whom I didn't recognize. All the new Arboretum volunteers had a sandwich. I myself had a roast beef sandwich," assured Crow.

"Which business?" asked Captain Moore.

"What?"

"Which downtown business made the sandwiches?"

"I'd have to look that up in my records. We have several different caterers," replied Crow.

Father and daughter exchanged a look.

"Who handled the sandwiches besides you?" Madeline asked, taking notes on all of Crow's responses.

"My new volunteer, Bebe Daniels, took all the sandwiches into the area designated for lunch and marked each one as I told her. I had called in the orders a couple days before the session, and as I remember, it came to five roast beef, three cheese and one peanut butter."

"And Rosenkraatz ordered the peanut butter, right?" questioned Michael.

"Yes," said Crow.

"Then the person who made them, the delivery boy, and Bebe Daniels are the only ones who handled the sandwiches?"

"As far as I know," said Crow.

"You said each one also had a soft drink . . . like Coke? In cans?" Madeline wanted to know.

"Right."

"And you had a Coke yourself?" asked Michael.

"Yes, and as far as I remember, so did all the volunteers."

"Is that all we need from Crow right now?" Michael asked his daughter, Madeline.

"That is all I can think of . . . but Mr. Crow, I assume you will be available to answer questions in the future?" said Madeline as she and her father rose to go.

"Do you think Ralph's death might be tied to the killing of the roses in the Arboretum on the same day," asked Crow.

"We knew nothing about the roses," said Michael.

"Go ahead with the story about your roses, Mr. Crow," said Madeline sitting back down.

"Two of my volunteers were absent some of the time during the slides," said Crow.

"You don't say?" said Madeline. "Who were they?"

"John Jones, Ernest Erickson's chauffeur, and Virginia Haynes, Erickson's secretary."

"Who is Erickson?" questioned Michael.

Both the Moores thought they saw a slight flush in the tone of Crow's skin.

"He owns a hotel or two in town," said Crow.

"You don't mean that Ernest Erickson, the hotel tycoon, is a volunteer for roses?" asked Madeline.

"We get all kinds of people," proudly commented Crow.

"Do you think Jones and Haynes might have killed the roses?"

"No, I don't, because they are the ones who reported the death of the shrub roses."

"Isn't it possible they might have reported the dead roses to take suspicion from themselves?" asked Madeline. Before she let Crow answer, the continued, "Why did they leave during the middle of the slide showing?"

"All I can tell you is that they were holding hands when they left. I believe they were more interested in each other than Rosenkraatz's slides."

Madeline suggested to Michael, "I think I'll take a walk to look at the dead roses to see if there are any clues there."

"Right." Moore was accustomed to Madeline going off on her own.

"Let me tell you . . . anyone who could kill roses wouldn't have trouble knocking off some..." volunteered Crow.

"Some what? Some phony expert on roses, perhaps?" asked Madeline.

When Crow had regained his composure, he replied, "You said it, Miss Moore, I didn't."

After that remark, Madeline went to see what happened to the shrub roses.

A secretary came in, handed a list to Crow, who handed it to Moore. After Crow gave Moore the volunteer roster, he handed him another slip of paper and said:

"Mr. Moore, here is something I think you should have in your investigation. It is a poem called "Sister Helen." Mr. Rosenkraatz had this in his hand when he died, along with a note."

"Why didn't you give this to the police earlier?" asked Moore.

"I didn't think it was a murder, then," said Crow.

Moore quickly read the note. "This means everyone in the room when it happened is a suspect. Did anyone else besides you touch this?"

Crow thought for a while. "Yes, the paramedic handed it to me."

Moore thought to himself that fingerprints would probably be out of the question after so many people had handled the evidence. "First of all I would like the name of the woman who marked all the sandwiches."

"You mean Bebe Daniels?" inquired Crow.

"If she is the one."

After Moore left the Arboretum, he called Bebe and made an appointment to see her that afternoon.

"See me in the reference room of the library," Bebe told Moore. So Moore went to the library.

The place was not unfamiliar to him.

Many an old movie he had checked out. He didn't like all the crime and violence in the movies of the 90's. He got enough of that in his job. So he was in the habit of picking up old classics at the library when he couldn't sleep. Before his interview with Bebe he looked for just one of the old Bebe Daniels movies, but could find none. He had a knack when dealing in crime to find a subject of mutual interest subject with his suspects. That way he could make them feel as if he were their friend. And many times it worked.

His library card was used more than his driver's license . . . or his Master Card.

Before Michael saw Bebe, he knew all about the silent movie star of the same name.

Michael took the elevator to the third floor. Here at the reference table, he introduced himself as a detective and asked where he could find Bebe Daniels.

There was some commotion in a side room. It

appeared that two young teenagers were kissing each other. The librarian fiercely reprimanded the boy.

"There is no kissing in the library. You can read about lovers all you want but you can't act like them here."

The receptionist pointed to the librarian who had just scolded the teenager. "There is Bebe Daniels," he said.

Michael walked up to Bebe cautiously and said, "May I have a few moments of your time. I am Michael Moore. I called because I wanted to speak with you about the death of Ralph Rosenkraatz."

"I assumed you would be coming around."

"I understand you marked the box lunches."

"Are you implying I had something to do with his death?" She meant her words to be just a whisper, but they echoed through the library.

"We are not accusing you of anything. This is just routine questioning of witnesses to a crime."

"I didn't know he was dead until I read about it in the paper."

"What happened until the paramedics arrived?"

"I thought I could handle this, but I don't think I can. Would you come to my house later?"

"Tell me where you live and I will," said Captain Moore.

"I reside in a two-story brown, stucco house on the corner of Albert and Bowen. Any time after 7 P.M." With this remark, Bebe spun away from Moore and returned to her corner in the library. As she stormed past Moore, he got a heavy scent of perfume and he thought to himself, although he knew nothing about perfumes, it sure smelled like a rose.

As Moore drove up Albert street about 7:00 P.M., he noticed a red Mustang parked in front of a one-car garage. The garage was separated from the house by a 15-foot-high lilac hedge. Thieves in the night could steal her Mustang and she would never hear nor see them.

Bebe had the outside door light on even though it was still light.

She had not given Moore the street number, but her house light was the only one on at the corner of Bowen. Two white pillars invited him to step up and ring the bell.

Bebe came to the door.

"Thanks for not driving up in a squad car with the lights flashing."

"I like your house. It has character," observed Moore. "Do you live here alone?"

"Very alone," said Bebe, who met him in a rose colored kimono. The aroma of roses permeated the air surrounding her.

"I have a cup of coffee for you."

"Excellent. I will take it."

Her living room window overlooked the street. In it, in a hurried glance, Moore observed a fireplace in marble.

Before Michael could sit down, Bebe walked over

to a wind-up phonograph, cranked it up and put a 78 record on it.

It was an old Bing Crosby 78 and, with Crosby singing "You're Getting to be a Habit with Me," Bebe pointed to a sofa for Moore to sit, then slid beside him.

When the music ended, Moore couldn't help saying, "Are you trying to suggest I'm getting to be a habit?"

"Not at all. My namesake, Bebe Daniels first sang that song, in one of the first talking pictures, *42nd Street*.

Moore replied, "I didn't know there was such a show."

"Most people who first meet me always ask, 'Where in the world did you get that name?'"

"I didn't come here, Miss Daniels, to hear how you got your name."

"You want to get right down to business," crooned Bebe?

"Something like that," said Moore.

"You want to know what I know about Rosenkraatz's death?"

"It's the same old question: Where were you when he got his peanut butter sandwich?"

"I am the one who gave him the sandwich." Bebe pouted.

"O.K. How did you get your name."

"My father was a teenager in the roaring 20's. The

only movies were silent pictures until the talkies came. He, as young boys often do, fell in love with a movie star. Her name was Bebe Daniels. Next to Gloria Swanson or Pola Negri, she was the most popular silent star. Her best silent pictures were *Fireman Save My Child, Nothing But Trouble,* and *Wild, Wild Sueö*. With leading man Rudolph Valentino, she co-starred in *Feel My Pulse."* With that, Bebe moved just a bit closer to Moore.

"When the talkies came in the late 20's, many silent stars disappeared because their voices surely didn't sound as good as the stars looked. But Bebe could sing. In fact, in *42nd Street,* Bebe had top billing over George Brent, Ginger Rogers and Una Merkel, but not over Ruby Keeler, the tap dancing star.

"My father, when young, developed a crush on this movie star and, much to my mother's disgust, he never got over it . . . so that is why I am called Bebe."

Moore realized how clever this woman was. Her best defense may have been to talk about another subject besides the murder.

"Can we discuss the event that took place at the Arboretum?" Moore said, trying to get the conversation back on track.

"What is it you want to know from me?" asked Bebe.

"Right now," he said as he stared into Bebe's eyes, "I would like to know what perfume you use." Moore appeared to be a little dizzy from the aroma.

"You like it?" laughed Bebe. "It is a favorite of mine and called Joy. It's the best perfume that money can buy, even better than Channel No. 5 or a rose scented perfume called Bernini."

Moore tried again to get back to the reason he made this call.

"Tell me, Miss Daniels, why did you give Rosenkraatz the peanut butter sandwich?"

"I gave it to him because that is what he ordered."

"So no one at the meeting touched that sandwich before you?"

"Bernard Crow told me to take the sandwiches from the delivery boy and mark each box."

"So no one handled them but you and, of course, the people who made the box lunches and the ones who delivered them?"

"As far as I know, that is correct. But that doesn't make me a murderer. I didn't even open the box."

Moore changed his tactics. "Had you ever met Rosenkraatz before this slide show?"

"Never in my life."

"What was your feeling about his presentation?"

"Very boring . . . not at all what we wanted to hear."

"And you wanted to hear?"

"What roses grow the best here in the North and how to take care of them over the winter months."

"Do you suspect any volunteers who might have wanted to kill him?"

"All I can say is, I didn't know any of the people in the room outside of Bernard Crow. How he ever got to be the curator, I'll never know."

"Why do you say that? Don't you like him?"

"He means nothing to me, if you know what I mean," said Bebe as she uncrossed and re-crossed her legs.

"No, I don't know what you mean," replied Moore.

"I just don't think Crow was the most qualified person for the position."

Moore was quite surprised at this turn in the conversation. Maybe the poison was meant for Crow? He'd have to look into that. But Bebe's perfume was getting to him and he wanted out. He felt that Bebe was not able to tell him any more about the Rosenkraatz killing.

"I have to get a report into the office. Would you excuse me, Miss Daniels?"

"Just a minute. I'll get your hat."

With that she leaned over him on the couch. When he left an hour later, he noticed the red Mustang once more.

Captain Moore and his daughter met as planned at the Green Mill restaurant on Grand and Hamline. Madeline always liked going to the Mill because of the pizza. Michael always ordered the soup.

A new waitress came to their booth.

"Let me make this perfectly clear. I do not want pizza," said Captain Moore.

"What?" the startled server asked.

Madeline whispered to Michael, "Watch what you say to this poor girl, she is new here. Everybody in the restaurant heard you shout to her what you didn't want. Now tell her what you do want."

"I will have the soup of the day if it isn't clam chowder," said Moore.

"It's Minnesota wild rice," said the server.

"That's fine," said Moore.

"Anything to drink?" asked the server.

"Just water," said Moore.

Turning to Madeline, the waitress smiled. "And what would you like."

"What would you suggest?" asked Madeline.

"Well, since 1976, we here at the Green Mill have been honored to receive over thirty awards for best pizza, so I would recommend one of our deep-dish pizzas."

"Which one?"

" To ensure proper cooking, we strongly suggest a maximum of five items,"

"Do you have any suggestions?" Madeline asked.

The waitress said, "My favorite is garlic and fresh tomato with either sausage or spicy chicken and black olives. Then I cap it all with smoked ham and goat cheese."

"That sounds great," said Madeline, "but I think I'll have a small cheese pizza and a diet coke."

The server gave her a puzzled look and then left.

"What did you find out about the roses? Are they all dead?" asked Moore.

"I went to all the different roses and found only one kind completely destroyed," answered Madeline.

"Tell me what you found?"

Madeline pulled a can out of her tote bag and held it with a rag.

"I found this can of Roundup in the ditch by the road near the shrub rose called the Bush rose. It's called the Bush rose because it has a bushy growth like the former President's wife's hair," explained Madeline.

"You mean Barbara Bush?"

"That's the one."

Captain Moore took the can and rag. He read, "When it kills the flower, it kills the roots."

"Right."

"If you don't think there's a connection between the rose and Rosenkraatz killings, then we might be wasting our time."

"What do you think?" asked Madeline.

"We have a double problem here Madeline. We have two murders: one a hex and the other a vex."

"What do you mean, Father? Hex and vex?"

"My first experience with vex goes back to the days of my youth. Halloween was our big vex day. It was not a day like today, when you knock on the door and say 'trick or treat.' In our Como neighborhood lived a cantankerous old man we called Daddy Long Legs.

"Each Halloween night we lifted an eighty-pound sewer cap from the street and dumped it on Daddy Long Legs' front door steps. Then we soaped his car windows with crayons!

"Only then did we ring his door bell and run. Out he came and stumbled over the sewer cap, got up and ran down the street looking for us vandals. Of course he never caught up with us because we hid under his tall lilac bushes. This trick we can call vexation, something we did just to annoy and irritate. I classify the burning of rose bushes a vex.

"Now hexing is another story, like the murder of Rosenkraatz. That is voodoo stuff, burning down wax candles, foretelling the end of Rosenkraatz.

"The murder of Rosenkraatz was obviously premeditated, but it doesn't appear to be for sex or money, so it must be for revenge."

Madeline interrupted, "How do you know it wasn't for sex or money?"

"Did you see the pictures of Rosenkraatz? He didn't seem the Romeo type."

"Remember, Father," interrupted Madeline, "the time a jealous husband, in a fit of insanity, tied his bowling bag with his bowling ball in it to his wife's legs and dropped her through a fishing hole in the local lake in the middle of winter?"

"Yeah," said Captain Moore. "That summer, the bag drifted ashore after it rotted away from the bowling ball. On the bag, police found the husband's initials and arrested him for murder."

"Both the husband and the wife's lover could have starred in before pictures in those weight loss ads," Madeline added.

Moore agreed. "You're right. Neither one of them were pretty boys, but as far as we can tell, Rosenkraatz hadn't been with a woman since he and Rosenkraatz's sister split up. In any case, killing someone in front of eight witnesses is pretty bizarre."

"What about the time a couple argued while they were traveling over the High Bridge in St. Paul," Madeline asked, "and the wife threw him into the water 150 feet below? Her story was that he was drunk and fell. Now that's bizarre."

"Maybe you're right," said Captain Moore. "This 'Sister Helen' thing seems pretty bizarre to me, though." He took the poem from his pocket.

"Did Bernard Crow give you that?"

"He did so reluctantly."

"Shouldn't that be in an evidence locker someplace?" Madeline asked.

"I'll take it there first thing in the morning. By the way, did you notice a catch in Crow's throat when he mentioned that magnate Ernest Erickson?"

Madeline thought. "Sure. Do you think it means anything?"

"I'm not sure." Moore swiveled in the comfortable booth. "I wonder where that soup is?"

"Not to change the subject, but be sure to take fingerprints from if you can, since we're obviously not going to get any from the letter," Madeline suggested.

"I doubt we'll catch the killer that way, but it's worth a shot. Maybe we'll get lucky. Ahhh," said Moore, "our luck's changed already. Here's our food."

Madeline smiled at the server and Moore grabbed his spoon.

"This doesn't seem like you're typical ritual murder," Moore said chewing a generous chunk of chicken. "But can't ignore these references to voodoo. In questioning the volunteers, we must look for the oddball ones with peculiar behavior."

Madeline was enjoying her pizza, but stopped chewing long enough to say.

"Any of the volunteers could have dug up this 'Sister Helen' poem at the library, especially the librarian, what was her name?"

"Bebe," said Moore, taking another large spoonful of wild rice.

"You didn't tell me about your interview with her," Madeline said with a wink.

"Bebe Daniels lives alone on the corner of Albert and Bowen. She has a red Mustang and an old record player."

"Is that all you found out?"

"She is jealous of the Bernard Crow. I know that much."

"What do you mean, jealous of Crow?"

"She thinks he's not qualified for his job," replied Captain Moore.

"Do you think that has anything to do with the murder?"

"Maybe, but I doubt it."

"Did you learn anything else?" asked Madeline.

"She has a tattoo of a red rose."

"Where?" asked a shocked Madeline.

"I'm not allowed to divulge that kind of information," said Moore, who then gave his daughter a wink, "but I don't think she's the murderer; at worst, she's the rose killer. How about Wendall Holmes? The Sherlock Holmes Society member. Or L.T. Bush, the novelist. They're both always looking for a new approach to a murder case? Maybe they just got carried away. Now, Madeline, I think it's time for you to interview our Mr. Bush."

With that, Moore dropped his spoon and wiped his mouth with his napkin.

Madeline drove her Volvo to the home of L.T. Bush. L.T. lived in the suburbs of St. Paul. His apartment had two bedrooms: one for sleep, one for his office. Security was solid. Special keys opened the apartment door, the garage door, and the pool door.

Madeline phoned Mr. Bush from the lobby. She explained who she was. L.T. reluctantly admitted her into the building.

"What do you want to see me for?" L.T. asked after he opened his apartment door.

Madeline entered his foyer. "I need to know all you saw at the Volunteer meeting when Mr. Rosenkraatz was killed."

"I saw very little."

"You are not aware that Mr. Rosenkraatz was poisoned?"

"I only know what I read in the morning paper."

"Mr. Bernard Crow has listed you as one of the participants in the session on roses."

"That is correct. I was there."

Madeline, getting tired of standing, said "What a lovely apartment. May I look around?"

"Can I offer you a cup of coffee?"

"Please do," answered Madeline as she followed L.T. into the kitchen.

"I assume you want it black. No cream. No sugar."

"Why assume that?"

"You had better have that gorgeous head of yours clear when you go out to get the killer. Coffee clears the head."

"Why, Mr. Bush. . . ," Madeline began.

"Call me L.T. Shall we?" He swept his arm in the direction of the living room. They both sauntered over to Duncan Phyfe sofa that had a view of downtown St. Paul far in the distance."

"You have nice apartment," Madeline said.

"Why, thank you."

Madeline thought to herself that if looks could kill, this guy wouldn't stand a chance in a fight to the death. He wore a heavy beard and had very merry blue eyes. Nothing sinister at all. In fact, he looked almost like Santa Clause.

Madeline saw his book *The Rose in Her Hair* lying on the table next to her. Wall Street Journals were stuffed into a rack of magazines. Above the door to the kitchen hung a banner from the University of Minnesota.

"You certainly have varied interests," observed Madeline. "Could I see your book? I noticed your name as the author."

"Here, I'll autograph it for you. For paying me this nice visit." L. T. signed the book with a flourish and handed it to her. Not to smudge his fingerprints, she placed it very carefully in her purse.

"I really didn't come to beg for this book."

"What did you come to beg for?"

"Just the facts."

"I did not kill Rosenkraatz. But frankly, I won't miss him."

"You are a crime novelist, or so I have heard. What do you think happened to him?"

"Somebody didn't like his name on their roses."

"What?" asked Madeline.

"Rosenkraatz was known to take liberties with other people's work on hybrids."

"One would have to have more motive than that to kill somebody, don't you agree?"

"How is your coffee?" asked L.T.

"Tasty," replied Madeline, well aware of how L. T. avoided the question.

"If I were to kill Rosenkraatz, I would have done it differently."

"What to you mean by that, Mr. Bush?" inquired Madeline.

Just then the phone rang.

L. T. answered. "One of them is here now. She says she helps her father on murder cases. I've told her nothing, of course. If she wants more, she'll have to speak with my attorney." He waited for a while then closed off with, "I'll be down to see you tomorrow . . . same place."

With that statement, L.T. set the phone down. "You police certainly get around in a hurry."

"Why do you say that?" asked Madeline.

"That was Bebe Daniels. Your father has been to see her on the Rosenkraatz murder.

"We are seeing everyone who was at the meeting. It's no secret. You are all suspects," lightheartedly added Madeline.

"But, as I already told you, that was no way to do away with Rosenkraatz," said L.T. "He deserved much worse."

Madeline didn't like his flippant attitude.

"What would you do on this case?"

"Find out who had reason to kill him."

"Sounds like you might have one," Madeline said.

"I didn't like the man, but it would be a waste of my time to murder him. Have you ever read Fyodor Dostoevski?" L.T. asked Madeline.

"The only book of his I've read is *Crime and Punishment*. It was required reading in my criminal justice classes at Inver Hills."

"I am rereading it for the second time. I am fascinated by his approach to the criminal mind. He maintains that the criminal always returns to the scene of the crime."

"Does that make sense to you?"

"If the murderer wants to remain a volunteer at the Arboretum, it means he or she *must* go back."

"Do you plan to go back?" Madeline asked.

L.T. laughed. "I need to go back. This incident will be a new novel for me."

"Will it be the story of a novelist returning to the scene of the crime?"

"Don't be insulting," L.T. said. "I had nothing to do with Rosenkraatz's death, but I think I do know who did it."

"Tell me."

"Here it is, exactly as I saw it. First of all, arsenic in a peanut butter sandwich did him in, right? That is the autopsy report I got from the coroner's office."

"Who put the arsenic in the sandwich, do you think?" asked Madeline.

L. T. Bush continued, "An unseen hand gave all the sandwiches to Bernard Crow. Crow then gave the sandwiches to Bebe Daniels to mark each one for proper identification. That makes Bernard and Bebe the primary suspects. Right so far?"

"You tell me. I wasn't there."

"After that, we each got our own sandwiches; no one touched anyone else's box. End of story."

"Not quite," Madeline said. "There is one thing not mentioned in the newspaper. Someone killed a section of roses. That person used a weed killer called Roundup. Any ideas on who might have done that?"

"No question in my mind," L. T. responded. "It had to be those two lovers who left the session hand in hand for a walk around the Arboretum."

"And who are they?" asked Madeline.

"They are close to Mr. Erickson, the hotel magnate. One is his chauffeur and the woman is his secretary."

"Why do you call him a magnate?"

"Magnate, mogul, industrialist, bigwig, big wheel, boss, captain of industry. Actually, tycoon comes from the ancient Chinese word for emperor. Perhaps that fits best."

"Sounds like you don't approve."

"Not at all," said L.T. "I just think a man as obviously bright as he is needs to hire smarter people, that's all. Virginia Haynes and John Jones both made it clear they didn't like roses."

"In any case," Madeline said, "we're mostly interested in who might have killed Rosenkraatz."

"We have eliminated me as the man who killed him, right?"

"No, I can't give you that assurance," Madeline said, then smiled. "Would you excuse me for a moment. May I use your bathroom?" asked Madeline.

"Certainly. Make yourself at home. It is the rose-colored room on the left down the hallway."

Madeline got up and went into the bathroom. She cautiously opened the medicine cabinet and looked it over. She found nothing out of the ordinary: Aqua Velva after shave lotion, Right Guard deodorant, Cool Mint Listerine antiseptic, Arm & Hammer Dental Care toothpaste, toothbrush, Band-Aids, Saline Nasal Spray. And then something startled her, a very beautiful box of perfume called Joy.

She shut the medicine cabinet, flushed the toilet and went back in the living room with L.T. On the way toward the living room, she spotted a small wax figure on the fireplace mantle.

"Is this a voodoo doll?" she asked L.T.

"It could be," acknowledged L. T.

"Have you ever heard of the poem 'Sister Helen,' Mr. Bush?" Madeline asked. She was beginning to suspect L. T. Bush as the culprit.

"No. I was a botany major, not an English major."

"Did you go to school with the deceased?" Madeline asked.

"Nice try. Iowa State. Class of '77. I believe ol' Rosie was an alum of dear old University of Minnesota. You just keep in touch with me on the murderer of the roses, and we'll solve it together," offered L.T.

She picked up her purse, smiled graciously at L.T. and said, "Good night. I will keep in touch." As she drove away, she caught a glimpse of a red Mustang driving up to L.T.'s apartment.

# Chapter Three

Michael Moore's next interview was with Rita Rosetta, the florist. He found her place of business very pleasant, just a short hop over the High Bridge from downtown St. Paul in a working class neighborhood of closely packed bungalows and family businesses.

A bell over the door announced his coming. Rita herself appeared from beneath an arch of flowers. She moved as quietly as a nun.

Rita's "Good Morning" was as soft and quiet as her step, as if she didn't want to disturb anyone sleeping in the area.

"May I introduce myself?" asked Moore.

"Please do. If you are here to make arrangements for a funeral, you will have to come back after 11:00 A.M. I personally don't handle funerals. I have an assistant who does that."

A customer came in. "Everything ready for Father Carlson, Sister?"

"Come back at eleven and I'll have it ready," Rita replied.

The customer left with a "Thanks" and a wave of the hand.

Moore couldn't help asking, "Is that your sister?"

"No, I used to be a nun and my friends still call me sister."

"I am with the Police Department, and I am questioning all the Arboretum volunteers who attended the showing of slides by Mr. Ralph Rosenkraatz, who, as you know, was murdered during the slide showing."

"Yes?"

"Bernard Crow gave me a list of all the new volunteers who were at that meeting."

"I cannot deny that I was there, but I had nothing to do with his murder, if that is why you are seeing me."

"I am here to find out from you what you saw happening that day."

"Would you mind stepping into my office?"

She led him through all the flowers into a very surprising looking office. To Moore, it looked like a garage sale of hats. He couldn't count the number of hats on display, but at least fifty would be his minimum guess.

"You look surprised by the hats?"

"Frankly, I am astounded."

"Don't be, there is a good reason for all of them."

"Please tell me more?"

"As you already know, I was once a nun. The order I belonged to required all of the nuns' heads and hair to be hidden under a different assortment of veils."

"Were you a School Sister of Notre Dame?"

"No, that was not the order."

"I only ask about SSND because I have a niece who is one. But go on," he said, nodding toward the hats.

"You will notice I have beautiful black hair?" Rita said, moving closer toward him, "and I want to show it off. Every time I take my hat off, I want people to say, 'Oh, what beautiful hair you have.'"

As she lifted her hair close to Moore, he said, "Oh, what beautiful hair you have."

Rita laughed.

Moore laughed, too, then asked, "What happened at that slide showing before Rosenkraatz took sick? Did anyone leave the show?"

"Of course, all the lights were off during the showing," explained Rita, "so if anybody left at any time, I might not have noticed."

"Did you leave?" asked Moore.

"I went out once to get a glass of water."

"Did anyone else that you know of leave at any time?"

"Just the two lovebirds," Rita said with a snort. "They went out while I was getting my water."

"Lovebirds?"

"That secretary and the chauffeur. They both work for that hotel guy."

"I have a Mr. Erickson on my list to be interviewed. Is he the guy?" asked Moore.

"Yes."

Moore continued, "What did you think of Rosenkraatz's presentation?"

"I thought it left a lot to be desired," Rita offered.

"You didn't like it?"

"I could have done better myself."

"How?"

Rita shot back, "He never once mentioned miniature roses. Not once. Tell me why?"

Moore backed away slightly. "I wasn't there. I wouldn't know."

"I'll tell you why. They are becoming more popular every day because people are beginning to recognize their charm. They are good for landscaping—ground cover, edgings, borders—and they can be grown indoors."

Moore started to feel as if he were back in school. "That's all very interesting," he said, "but I really just want to know about what happened the day of the murder of Rosenkraatz. Did you...."

"Allow me to finish what I am saying about miniatures," interrupted Rita. "I will tell you how he got poisoned when I am through with the miniatures; then I will tell you who I think did the man in."

Moore decided he could stand a few more rose lessons to hear her hunch, so he relaxed and waited.

Rita took one of the many hats off the rack and went to a mirror to put it on. "How do you like this hat? I just got it yesterday at Dayton's," Rita said as she spun around to face Moore.

"Looks great," said Moore, trying to show more enthusiasm than he felt.

"Miniatures make fine indoor plants. Put them near a window away from the hot sunlight and be sure to feed them regularly and, before I forget, wash the foliage in the sink every week or two to keep insects at bay. And now I bet you want to know the best miniatures to grow?"

Moore nodded his head.

"My Valentine is a lovely red, Popcorn is a dandy white, Baby Darling has pink-apricot flowers. Other good miniatures? Yellow Doll, Orange Honey and Dreamglo. Now let's review the crime. . . ."

Moore was thinking to himself that it was fortunate that Rita didn't decide to try on more of her hats.

"It has been established by the coroner's office that Rosenkraatz died from an overdose of arsenic in a peanut butter sandwich, has it not?"

"Did everyone in the city think they knew about this?" wondered Moore.

"First of all," Rita began, "the person who made the sandwiches could have put poison in the peanut butter, but how would he have known for whom that particular sandwich was intended? Next, the delivery person who handed the sandwiches to Bernard Crow through the door while we were watching the slides could have done it, but we would have to ask the same question. Then Mr. Crow handed the sandwiches to Bebe Daniels to mark each box. Crow didn't have the boxes long enough to put poison on anything. That leaves Bebe. I ordered beef and got it from Bebe. Then we all went to a makeshift dining room and ate. After that, we helped ourselves to a Coke."

"Were all the box lunches closed when you first saw them?"

"Yes," replied Rita.

"Did you notice if any of the boxes had been tampered with?"

"All I can tell you is that mine wasn't," said Rita.

"So as far as you know then, the only people to touch Rosenkraatz's box was the person who made it, the delivery person who handed it to Crow, Bebe Daniels and Rosenkraatz himself?"

"That is all I can tell you, except that Crow doesn't have the nerve to kill a bug, let alone a man," Rita said, "so that leaves that little hussy Bebe Daniels."

"Why do you call her a hussy?" Moore asked.

"You tell me, detective," answered Rita. "I presume you've already interviewed her."

Moore blushed slightly, then regained his composure enough to ask, "What, pray tell me, was her motive?"

"Jealousy, I suppose," Rita said with a yawn. "She was jealous of Rosenkraatz's stature in the field of roses."

"Thank you. I think that's enough for now," Moore said.

Rita smiled and extended her hand, showing a beautiful set of teeth. "Stop by any time, officer," she said.

"I may just do that," Moore said as he walked out the door of the floral shop.

Moore headed for Snuffy's Malt Shop at St. Clair and Cleveland for a meeting with Madeline.

"I'll have the soup of the day, as long as it's not clam chowder," Moore said as he stood in line before Madeline arrived.

"No," said Ray, "Wednesday is chicken noodle."

"Fine," said Moore.

He sat at the table and sipped his soup waiting for Madeline. When she arrived, she was the first to speak: "How did you do with the flower arranger?"

"I know more about miniature roses than I know about who murdered Rosenkraatz," said a smiling Moore.

"Roses again?"

"Yeh, it seems all our suspects were into roses in a big way, and with Rita Rosetta you can add hats to that list."

"Why hats?"

"You have heard of people who collect string? Well, Rita collects hats because she once was a nun whose head was always covered. So she continues to keep it covered." Moore changed the topic. "She thinks that the killer of Rosenkraatz was Bebe Daniels."

"And why Bebe?"

"Rita claims Bebe knew more about roses than Rosenkraatz, and was jealous of his popularity in the world of roses."

"That seems like a weak motive for killing anyone. Don't you agree?"

"Yes, I agree, but the first thing they teach 'em in law school is that motive has nothing to do with it."

"Bebe seems more like a candidate for killing the roses," observed Madeline.

"By the way, the department's checking the fingerprints you got from L. T. Bush to see if we can find a match."

"Keep me informed."

"Hey, the soup here is pretty good. You ought to have some," said Moore.

"I'm not hungry right now," said Madeline.

"Fine, I just wanted to share this great cuisine with you. Anyway, I want you to visit another volunteer," Moore said to his daughter.

"Who is that?" inquired Madeline.

"Wendell Holmes."

"Is he a bike ride away from here or a Volvo ride?"

"Either a long bike ride or a short Volvo ride. He lives by Como Lake."

"Give me his street address and I'll see him tomorrow."

"I want to caution you about your visit with Wendall Holmes," said Moore.

"Why?" asked Madeline. "Is he dangerous?"

"Maybe."

"What do you know?"

"I know that he has been a patient at the St. Peter Asylum for the insane," said Moore. "He has been diagnosed as a schizophrenic."

"What else did you find out?"

"They tell me that as long as he is on medication he is normal," Moore replied. "But if he forgets to take his medication, he may suffer from delusions and hallucinations."

"The kind of eccentric behavior that could mean sending an intended victim messages warning him of impending doom?"

"You mean the 'Sister Helen' message?" asked Moore.

"Exactly what I mean," said Madeline.

"I thought the same thing. That's why I want you to be careful."

"Well, I'll keep my eyes open with Holmes," Madeline agreed.

Moore's last words to Madeline as she left were, "Are you sure you wouldn't like a chocolate malt?"

Madeline laughed as she walked to her car.

Holmes' apartment overlooked a small golf course northwest of Como Lake. Madeline found Holmes' house in excellent repair although relatively old. She parked her Volvo in front of the house, went to the door, and rang the bell.

A gray-haired man in a turtleneck sweater and red scarf opened the door.

"What can I do for you, young lady?" he asked.

"I'd like to ask you a few questions about the murder at the Arboretum."

"Well, right now I am on my way for my daily walk around Lake Como. Would you care to join me so we can discuss it at length?" said Holmes.

"I'd be happy to walk with you. I need the exercise myself."

Down the hill the two went toward the path around the Lake. "This walk covers 1.8 miles. Is that o.k. with you?" asked Holmes.

"No problem," replied Madeline.

As they walked, Madeline spoke up again. "My father, Captain Moore, tells me you were at the slide showing by Mr. Rosenkraatz, at which time Mr. Rosenkraatz became ill and later died. Do you remember if anyone from the group left the meeting at any time?"

"A father/daughter team, eh?" Holmes said. "Now that would make an interesting mystery novel."

"I don't know that we'd be very good," Madeline said.

"That depends upon the author," Holmes insisted. "In any case, I recall the two lovers left in the middle of the showing."

"Lovers?" inquired Madeline.

"Lovers," Holmes repeated. "At least you might think that. They held hands and gave *soulful* looks into each other's eyes. But they were gone long enough to tell us that someone killed the roses. They had nothing to do with handing out the sandwiches, which I understand contained the poison that did Mr. Rosenkraatz in."

Madeline wondered the same thing as her father: "Did someone print the autopsy report on the front page of *Pioneer Press,* fer cryin' out loud?"

"Is that all you can tell me?" asked Madeline.

"That's all I can remember, sweetheart," Holmes said.

"I'm not your sweetheart," cautioned Madeline.

"We could work on that," said Holmes with a laugh.

Madeline picked up the pace.

"This walk should take us thirty-three minutes, Miss Moore," Holmes said. "At your pace we will be around the lake in twenty minutes. What's your hurry?"

Madeline tossed back her strawberry blonde hair and said, "I'm trying to break down your defenses."

By this time, the two had reached the Pavilion, a large building with many pillars. It served as an entertainment center for Lake Como and attracted thousands of people to its coffee shop and free concerts.

Here Holmes stopped to catch his breath.

"Here is where my desire to sing was fulfilled. Back

in the good old pavement dance days, the band leader needed a good singer to keep the marathon dancers awake, and I haven't stopped singing since," Holmes said.

He continued talking about his personal experiences at Como, for a while avoiding any questions about who killed the roses. "Here, years ago, the Olympic committee came to scout for speed skaters for the Winter Olympics. I almost qualified for the 5000 meter but slipped and fell on the last turn. It was about that time that Shipstead and Johnson were starting their Ice Capades shows. They wanted me, but I told them I could speed skate and figure skating was for girls."

Madeline thought that if they took the pronoun "I" out of the language, Holmes would be a ventriloquist's dummy!

"They stopped dog racing around the lake when my dog Earl ran away with all the races," continued Holmes with his amazing résumé.

Madeline quickly interrupted, "Can we get back to the killer for a minute?"

"What do you want to know about the killer?" Holmes asked as he bent over and brushed a small bit of dirt off his shoes.

"I want to know if you have any ideas?"

"Let me tell you of my experiences with hexes," said Holmes.

"Who said anything about a hex?" asked Madeline.

"What else could it be? Everyone loves roses, right? So, no one would just kill roses because they didn't like roses. Right?"

Before Madeline could agree or disagree, he continued: "I was a standout baseball pitcher in my youth. Every sports fan in Como will testify to that. I was a major league prospect at only seventeen. I played here in this area with an American Legion team and went with them to California for the national playoffs. It was my pitching that took us there and, as you know, baseball is ninety percent pitching. Right?"

While he took a deep breath to continue on his favorite subject. Madeline interrupted with a question: "Why do you think the killing of the roses was a hex?"

"I'll tell you why. I had a hex put on me once."

"When was that?" a now curious Madeline asked.

"I was about to pitch for the American Legion championship. The night before the big game, I found a dead cat in my bedroom in the hotel our team was staying at in L. A."

"How terrible," said Madeline. "Do you see any connection between killing roses and voodoo?"

By this time the two walkers were about half way around the lake, and Madeline was no longer racing, but her mind was.

"It was a warning to Rosenkraatz that his time was up, just like that dead cat in my room before the big game. It frightened me so much I couldn't find my best pitch that day . . . my knuckle ball. We lost the game."

"Who did it?" asked Madeline.

"No doubt in my mind . . . the Chinese coach of the West Coast team, the team that went on to win the national...."

"No," Madeline interrupted. "I mean who killed the roses? Do you know?" Madeline moved closer to Holmes awaiting his answer.

"Certainly. It was the two lovers. Remember they came in with the news about the killing. They're the only ones who had the time." Holmes leaned over and brushed dirt off his jacket, like Pontius Pilate washing his hands of the whole affair. "How do you stand on this rose bush killing?" asked Holmes of Madeline.

"I don't know yet," Madeline replied honestly. "By the way, why did you go to Rosenkraatz's slide show?"

"Years ago I wrote a musical comedy about the St. Paul Winter Carnival. I got nowhere with it, even though at the time, I knew the King of the Carnival. And, in the musical, a rose was mentioned in a song I wrote. Do you want to hear the story?"

"Not particularly."

"But it explains my presence at the lecture."

Madeline looked skeptical, but told him to go on.

"Here is the plot. A beautiful woman becomes Queen of the Winter Carnival. Under the rules of the pageant, she can't get married for one year. Her boyfriend, the mayor of St. Paul, doesn't want to wait a year and sings...."

At this point, Holmes cleared his throat and began

in a slightly flat rendition of his song: "What lover can wait a year / as you have asked me to do. / To wait and shed no tear, / if you can, then your love is not true. / Will you be here at the end of the year/ and love me then as ever? / Or will you be gone like the stars at the dawn / for a year is forever. / The rose shall be dead and its petals all shed." He stopped the song to interject a comment. "You see, she has a rose in her hair when he sings her the song."

Madeline managed to scrap up a painful smile.

He finished with a flourish of arms. "And bloom again will it never / for love is a fire, a flame of desire, / and a year would be forever."

Madeline was stunned and would have floated to the top of the lake if she were a fish.

"This musical comedy I wrote went before the Carnival Committee and a man named Rosenkraatz didn't like it. So I go to this slide showing just to see what this clown looks like; and frankly, I didn't like his looks, but I didn't kill him nor the roses."

By this time, the twosome had reached the end of their walk and started back to Holmes' house.

Although Madeline was not taken in by any of Holmes' show, she was inclined to agree with him about who killed the roses. Yet she knew the obvious answer was not always the correct answer. As they turned onto Holmes' street, he started to hum a tune. After a minute, he asked,

"Madeline, can you guess what it is?"

"Sure, that is 'Mexicali Rose.'"

And then Holmes hummed another tune.

"That is an easy one, too. 'Rosemarie.' Right?"

"Right. Try this."

"That's 'My Wild Irish Rose.'" Despite herself, Madeline was starting to enjoy Holmes' little game. She played the piano, but not too often. She had inherited some sheet music from her grandmother, so she knew these standard tunes from her small collection of piano sheet music. As they came near to Holmes' house he asked,

"Come on in and listen to my 78's?"

"What's that?" asked Madeline.

"Oh, you must come in! I'll show you."

Madeline was attracted by his enthusiasm for whatever it is he wanted to show her.

They reentered his house and he took her to a corner where stood a gleaming piece of wood furniture that Madeline would have guessed to be a liquor cabinet. When Holmes opened it, she saw some knobs, something that looked like an old phonograph, and some black, hard plastic disks.

"My grandmother left me this player and the records." Music started coming from the machine, scratchy and distant.

"Anything else your good old grandmother left you?"

"Well, if you really want to know, she left me her rocking chair. It didn't have money in it, but she left me a bank account that allows me a great deal of freedom."

"Freedom from what?" asked Madeline.

"Freedom from work."

"How did your grandmother get her money?" Madeline continued.

"Grandfather bought stock in 3M."

"So you made it the hard way," Madeline offered.

"I don't apologize for what I have, why should I?"

Madeline was getting to Holmes.

Holmes next put on "The Rose of Tralee," by John McCormick. Madeline thought it was wonderful in a corny way. For the moment, she forgot who killed the rose bushes.

Holmes sat next to Madeline on the couch and attempted to put his arm around her. This was a mistake.

"Back to the roses, Holmes, please. Put the fat lady on next."

"You mean the show is over?"

"You got that right, but my father and I will keep in touch until both murders are solved."

"Both murders?"

"Yes. The rose murder and the Rosenkraatz murder." Without any father comment, Madeline strode toward the door.

As she left, Holmes cried, "I sure like that Volvo. You'll have to give me a ride in it sometime. Let us have lunch some day and I will tell you how I am ahead of my time. We will discuss the book, *The End of Work* by Jeremy Rifkin. I will tell you how I am ready for the end of work."

Without looking back, Madeline gave a little wave, squeezed into her car, and sped away.

She drove north a couple blocks, turned left onto Larpenteur, and swung into the strip mall's parking lot.

She found Michael in Snuffy's, a joint with greasy burgers and thick malts.

"I'm having the chicken soup," Michael said to his daughter. "It's great here."

Madeline looked at a menu. "I'll have the Snuffy Burger."

After the server left, Moore asked, "How did you do with Wendall Holmes?"

"He has 'I' trouble,' Madeline said with a laugh.

"Eye trouble?"

"Yea. I couldn't get him off his favorite subject: himself. Even after a walk around Como Lake he was thinking about himself, but he did admit he didn't like Rosenkraatz."

"You don't think he killed the bushes?"

"No, but he claims he knows who did."

"Who?"

"He says the chauffeur and Erickson's secretary."

"Aren't they the ones who discovered the dead roses?"

"Yes, but they could have done the dirty work and claimed they discovered it to throw everyone off."

"I'll buy that," Moore said.

Moore's soup came and he dug in with gusto, cracking saltines into the mix to add some heft to the tasty broth.

"Did you see that article on biometrics in the paper?" he asked between bites.

"No," Madeline said, wishing her burger would arrive.

"According to this article, personal identity can now be used as a security system through Biometrics. As close as I can come to the understanding of Biometrics is that it scans a person's unique physiological and behavioral characteristics."

"For example?"

"For example," Moore answered, "fingerprinting, eye patterns, hand scans, signatures, voice verification, typing rhythms, facial features and statistical correlations of the geometric shape of a face."

Madeline's burger came, and she added ketchup to it before grabbing it with both hands, the grease making the bun stick to the wrap in the bottom of the plastic basket.

"I wouldn't waste any more time checking out Holmes," Moore finally said.

Madeline, used to her father's jumps in subject, simply asked "Why?"

"For the simple reason he has no motive to kill roses. Right?"

"Why do you say that?"

"The roses were most closely associated with Crow, the curator, and Erickson. Even if Holmes disliked Rosenkraatz enough to do something, why attack him that way? The destruction of the roses doesn't get to Rosenkraatz."

"Holmes thinks it was some sort of a hex, a warning."

"I doubt that," Moore said finishing.

Madeline continued to devour her burger in silence. "Where to next?" she asked chewing her last bite.

"I am giving you a tough one, Virginia Haynes, Ernest Erickson's secretary. And don't be too easy on her. I talked to Crow, and he said she is all business."

"I see you smiling. Was the soup that good?"

Michael picked up the bill and paid as they left Snuffy's.

The next day Madeline went to see Virginia at her place of business. A sparkling chandelier hung over the reception room of Erickson and Erickson. The E and E Building (as it was referred to by the local townspeople) was located on the busiest street in town. It covered one city block, about a soccer field long and a football field wide. The lobby held a life-size painting of Erickson himself, in oil, of course, and surrounded by a gilded frame. The other walls held pictures of other Ericksons.

Madeline could see Virginia coming down the hall to the reception area.

"I understand you're working with Captain Moore on the Arboretum case," said Virginia, not mincing any words. "Why are you here to see me?"

"I'm seeking your help in determining who killed the rose bushes at the Arboretum the day Mr. Rosenkraatz was killed," Madeline answered.

"What makes you think I would know anything?"

"You were there, weren't you?"

"Yes, I was at the slide showing by Mr. Rosenkraatz," Virginia agreed.

"Did you leave this showing at any time?"

"Mr. Jones and I left the slide showing for a breath of fresh air."

"I suppose you just went for a stroll among the flowers . . . the real flowers; were they more interesting than a slide?" asked Madeline.

"No, that was not the reason. Mr. Erickson's chauffeur, John Jones, went with me on what you called a stroll. I wanted him to see the beautiful assortment of rose bushes that Mr. Erickson had contributed to the Arboretum."

"What happened then?"

"We discovered the bushes were destroyed."

"And then?"

"Johnny and I hurried back to tell the curator, Bernard Crow,"

"And then?" Madeline repeated.

"Right after the announcement about the dead roses, we had lunch."

"And what did you have for lunch?"

"I had what I asked for earlier . . . a fine beef sandwich."

"And Rosenkraatz had . . . ?"

"Peanut butter—I remember that vividly because he was the only one who had a peanut butter sandwich."

Madeline was taking notes and was quiet for a while.

"Is that all you wanted to know?" Virginia asked impatiently.

"For the time being it is," responded Madeline.

"Am I a suspect?" Virginia asked.

Before Madeline would reply, Johnny Jones came over and stood next to Virginia. "Any trouble here, Virginia?"

"Johnny, I want you to meet . . . What is your name again?"

"Madeline Moore," said Madeline shaking Jones' hand.

"She is here investigating the murder of the roses at the Arboretum on the day Ralph Rosenkraatz was killed."

"What has that to do with you?" Jones asked, a little too much irritation showing in his voice.

"I believe she and her father think the murder of the roses and the killing of Rosenkraatz tie in together. Right, Madeline?" Haynes asked staring directly into Madeline's eyes.

"I never said that at all, Ms. Haynes."

"Virginia, er, Ms. Haynes and I discovered the dead rose bushes. That's all," Jones jumped in.

"I have one question," Madeline began, ignoring Jones. "Were these particular rose bushes of any importance that either of you were aware of?"

"Everyone knows that Mr. Erickson donates his own rose bushes to the Arboretum every year. It's a beautiful section of roses that stays alive here in the North Country through the winter," answered Virginia.

Jones added, "Virginia doesn't mean that they bloom all winter, of course."

"I didn't know you were a rose expert, Mr. Jones," Madeline said.

Jones bristled a little, but Virginia patted his arm.

"Now that Mr. Jones is here, I'd like to hear his version about how you two discovered the dead rose bushes."

"Virginia and I got bored with all that rose history and stupid songs, so we took a walk for our own intermission."

Virginia changed the subject by asking Jones, "How is the boss today? You brought him in a little late."

Jones replied, "He's still mad as hell over the burned bushes.

"He'll blame Crow for poor security, wait and see," cautioned Virginia.

Madeline took all this company talk in quietly, but

couldn't help asking, "Why would he be after the curator, Crow?"

"He has to blame somebody," Virginia said.

"Why?"

Haynes and Jones looked at one another, and finally Virginia spoke, "He's not about to let this go unpunished," Haynes said. "In Mr. Erickson's world, there is always a guilty party."

"You can say that again," Jones said, "Why one, that rotten...."

Haynes shot Jones a dirty look and he shut up. Madeline got the idea that was between the two of them, Haynes would be the leader in any plot, either killing roses or killing rose experts.

"Mr. Jones, what did you do after you discovered the roses?" Madeline asked.

"We both hurried back to the lecture to tell everyone?"

"Did you see anything unusual? Or anyone that was suspicious?" Madeline continued.

Haynes and Jones exchanged glances again, but neither could remember anything about their walk that was out of the ordinary, other than finding the dead roses.

"Thank you for your time," said Madeline as she left. She returned to her office to file a few reports, then went home to relax before starting another day.

The next day Michael was waiting at Huong Sen on Grand Avenue.

"What's new?" was his opening greeting to Madeline. "Have you solved the mystery of the killer of the rose bushes?"

"I have, indeed," smartly answered Madeline.

"Who did it?"

"John Jones and Virginia Hayes together."

"You have the evidence?"

"I have the guilty ones, but not the evidence, yet."

The server came with a big bowl of soup for Moore and took Madeline's order. "You should try the soup sometime. It's the best 'Hot and Sour' in the Twin Cities," Moore said.

"I'll take your word for it," Madeline said as she looked a the bowl the size of half a bowling ball piled high with vegetables and shrimp.

"So you think the driver and the secretary did in the roses," Moore said.

"No doubt in my mind," said Madeline.

"There's only one problem," Moore said.

Madeline asked, "What's that?"

Moore continued, "Remember the fingerprints you took from L.T. Bush?"

"Yes, what about them?" asked Madeline.

"I'm told the fingerprints on the Roundup can belong to L.T. Bush."

Moore let Madeline gather in the new information while he worked on his soup with a spoon that looked like a miniature frying pan.

"Why in the world would L.T. Bush kill bushes?"

"Maybe he just likes hexes. Remember the Viking

quarterback who thought he was hexed when he broke his toe in a scrimmage and was out for five games?"

"I don't follow sports the way you do," answered Madeline.

"It doesn't matter. I want you to re-visit Mr. Bush. You will have to confront him with this information," ordered Moore.

Madeline was not happy about another visit with Bush, but she held her tongue. "How are you coming on the murder of Rosenkraatz? Any hot leads?" she asked.

"None."

Madeline's spring rolls arrived. She asked for extra peanut sauce. "So everyone is still a suspect? Even with this new information about Bush?"

"We don't have any indication that the two crimes are related," Moore responded. "So we need to assume everyone is a suspect."

"What about the curator? You don't suspect that he would call the slide meeting to eliminate Rosenkraatz in front of all the volunteers?" asked Madeline.

"It's possible," Moore said, "although why he would wait all these years after Rosenkraatz and his sister divorced makes it unlikely. He had Rosenkraatz over to speak on numerous occasions. It wouldn't make sense to kill him now."

"Who is next in line?" anxiously asked Madeline.

"The next person to be taken off the suspect list is Rita Rosetta," said Moore.

"And why is Rita no longer a suspect?" asked Madeline, a little suspiciously.

"As you know, she runs a floral shop. She wears slippers at work so as not to disturb the flowers."

"You must be kidding!" Madeline said, smiling.

"She won't handle funerals. She takes care of only weddings and anniversaries. I checked it out. Apparently she's telling the truth on that one. She hires an assistant to make the floral arrangements for funerals," explained Moore.

"So you think someone who hates funerals and is nice to flowers couldn't be a killer?" joked Madeline.

"That's not all," Moore said taking a large gulp of soup. "Hold on to your hat, or her hat, if you prefer: she used to be a nun."

"I remember the one I had in grade school," Madeline said. "She was very handy with a foot ruler across your knuckles. It wouldn't surprise me if she had some skeletons buried under the convent floor."

Moore ignored this last remark. "Then we have Mr. L.T. Bush. If he could kill the roses, why not Rosenkraatz?"

"He admitted he didn't like Rosenkraatz," Madeline added.

"As did Jones and Haynes, according to you," said Moore.

"So we can't eliminate them," Madeline agreed. "What about Bebe Daniels?"

Moore stopped eating his soup for a moment. "It's

possible. I suspect she has enough *passion* to commit murder."

Madeline ignored his comment and continued. "That leaves Holmes. He's probably too self-absorbed to think about killing anyone else, but he does hold a grudge against Rosenkraatz for not publishing his musical."

"Did you tell him to get over it?" Moore asked.

"I didn't have the heart," said Madeline. "He obviously thought it was pretty good."

"Well, I hope you have the heart to put the heat on Bush."

"I'll leave him burning," replied Madeline as she rose to leave the restaurant while Moore finished his soup.

# Chapter Four

The night after the murder of Rosenkraatz, E.E. Erickson had worked late and, as usual, Virginia had remained behind to help. After a late session, they had headed for the Lexington and a late supper.

After parking his Cadillac in the alley entrance, Erickson opened the back door of the Lex and dutifully Virginia led him to the front door where a perky greeter led them to their usual spot in the back part of the dining room.

Before Haynes could sit down, E.E. moaned, "I'd like to kill the guy who killed my roses."

"That is not a Christian way to talk about someone who merely killed some flowers," said Virginia.

"Those were my special flowers, and you know it."

"But we were not yet sure those roses would be the ones that lasted longer and survived the cold better," Virginia pointed out.

"I had a feeling about them, though," Erickson said. "I felt sure with this bunch we were on to something."

Just then the server came to take their drink orders and tell them the specials of the night, finishing up with "and, as usual, we have the halibut teriyaki."

"I'll have a vodka martini," said Erickson, "and for you, Virginia."

Virginia ordered a slow gin fizz.

E.E. asked, "How are you and Johnny Jones getting along?"

"Why do you ask?"

"You looked pretty cozy at the Arboretum meeting."

"We just got tired of hearing all about roses, didn't you?"

"I never can hear enough about roses," E.E. replied.

Virginia changed the subject. "Where is Johnny Jones tonight?"

"I let him go home early tonight so he could go bowling."

Virginia said, "He surely likes bowling, and tells me his average is about one eighty."

Erickson teased, "Do you think, Virginia, that you and Jones could eventually go down the bowling lane together?"

Virginia patted E.E.'s hand. "Have no fear of my ever leaving you, E.E."

"You could still stay in your present capacity should you find your heart's desire."

The server came back with the drinks, and Erickson said he would have the halibut. "And for you, Virginia?"

"I'll have the same as Mr. Erickson."

"Thank you," the server said, I'll be right back with some bread.

Once the server left, E.E. said, "Many is the time I told you, Virginia, that you must have common interests. That is the only way with any prospective fiancé."

Virginia did not like this fatherly advice, well meant as it was. "The only common interest I have is my work with you, and it has taken up half my life so far."

Erickson was surprised by the sudden shift in Virginia's tone.

"You have been well paid, have you not?"

"Relatively."

"I have never mistreated you, have I?"

"Not deliberately."

Although he was curious why Virginia was less than enthusiastic about her working conditions, Erickson decided he was too tired to go further down that road and stuck to the one he had originally taken.

"Let me tell you once again about common interests. My wife and I play bridge; that is a common interest. Right?"

"If you both share an equal enthusiasm for the game," Virginia offered.

Erickson let this observation pass without comment. "What do you have in common with Jones? I am curious."

"I hate bowling; he loves it. He drinks 3.2 beer; I like champagne. He likes hockey; I prefer figure skating. He likes the Vikings; I support Green Bay because my mother was born in Milwaukee. I like to get up early in the morning; he likes to sleep late." With this last comment, Virginia smiled.

"How do you know he likes to sleep late in the morning?" questioned E.E.

"Because he told me so," said Virginia in a teasing voice.

"You are too smart to get involved with this beer swilling, Friday night bowling oaf," a disgusted Erickson said.

"You must admit he is a good chauffeur," said Virginia, glad to see that perhaps Erickson was just a little jealous.

"Anybody can be a good chauffeur. All it takes is a driver's license."

"What do you think I should I look for in a man?" said Virginia, leaning closer to Erickson.

"With your attributes, here is what the man should have for you: first a home on the River Boulevard, with a built-in garage so in the winter you would never have go outside; you would just get in your car and come to the executive E.E. building where you would park inside, dine in our deluxe dining room and drive home, never being exposed to the cold, cold Minnesota weather. How does that sound?"

"Wonderful," cried Virginia. "All I need is you."

Virginia grasped E.E.'s hand, which he withdrew quickly. "We've been all through that," Erickson said. "I slipped once, but I will not leave my wife." He quickly changed the subject. "Now getting back to the roses. What is this trouble we seem to be having in Portland on the rose gift for advanced reservations?"

Before Virginia could answer, their server brought their drinks and some bread. Erickson grabbed a chunk and slathered it with butter. "The problem in Portland with roses is that Portland is the 'city of roses.' Roses are as common as corn in Iowa or magnolias in Louisiana. I think we should substitute lilies."

"Good enough, Virginia," said E.E. chewing his bread. "Get in touch with our Portland manager and substitute lilies and remind me to give you a raise in the next quarter."

"I have put it down already along with one for John Jones too."

"Why should I give Jones a raise?"

"Can you get a better chauffeur?"

"I might not be able to buy a better golf swing,

although it would be easy to get a better chauffeur," said a smiling E.E. Erickson.

"Speaking of golf, your club called and the secretary told me you are up for the presidency," Virginia said.

"Not if I can help it. There are too many members who know how the club should be run. I am too busy with my roses. Come to think of it, I should put a rose garden out there by the 18th green."

The server brought their meals and stopped any more talk about roses. While eating, Virginia noted a few familiar faces in the room.

"I see two of the volunteers from the Arboretum over there," she said nodding toward the room behind Erickson. "Don't turn around; they'll notice you."

"How in the hell can I see them if I don't turn around?" he said partially turning in his chair.

"Don't," Virginia pleaded. "Wait until we leave and then look. To curb your curiosity, I will tell you the two: the Arboretum curator, Bernard Crow, and Bebe Daniels."

"Aren't those the two who gave out the sandwiches?" asked E.E.

"Exactly, E.E.," whispered Virginia. "What do you think of that?"

"Well," said E.E., "I wouldn't take a peanut butter sandwich from Bebe Daniels."

That made both of them laugh for a brief moment. When Virginia had stopped chuckling, she asked,

"What makes you think she had any reason to kill Rosenkraatz?"

"I don't know anything about that lady except that she gave out all the sandwiches, including the one to Rosenkraatz, and she was in that room by herself, as I remember."

Virginia, busy watching Bebe and Bernard, said, "Bebe is grabbing Crow's hands, but he pulls them away."

"Maybe he doesn't want her to show any affection. I know that feeling," E.E. said.

"What feeling is that?" asked a frowning Virginia.

"A desire not to give someone the wrong impression," Erickson said, then continued. "Before I forget it, call that curator and ask him what roses we should plant in place of those destroyed."

In disbelief, Virginia asked, "Do you mean you are going to keep sponsoring your rose garden at the Arboretum in spite of what happened?"

"We just have to find out who the rose killer is, then there won't be any more problems," Erickson said, taking another forkful of the fish.

"What will happen to a rose killer, do you think?" Virginia teased.

"He'll go to jail for vandalism, to teach him a lesson," Erickson said with conviction.

"What if it's a woman?"

"You know what I mean," Erickson growled.

"So how do propose catching the dastardly villain?"

Erickson missed the sarcasm in Haynes' voice.

"Here is how we will find the bastard," advised E.E. "We'll ask Crow which one of his gardeners was out working the day of the catastrophe. Certainly one of his caretakers must have seen what was going on."

"Don't you think the police have already done that?"

"They're too busy worrying about who killed Rosenkraatz to work on the real tragedy. In fact, I think I'll ask Crow this minute."

Erickson wiped his mouth with his napkin and began to rise.

Virginia reached over and touched him. "Don't ask him now while he is with that woman. For all we know, she might be the culprit."

"As usual, you're right, Virginia. I'll just...."

Virginia interrupted, "They're getting ready to leave. She is paying the bill."

"They must not pay those curators much," observed E.E.

"Not everyone is as generous as you are, E.E.," said Virginia.

"Well, as I'm sure you're well aware, 'Yes, Virginia, there is a Santa Claus.'" Erickson chortled loudly at his own wit. "Come to think of it, though, I don't think a librarian makes much money, either. So why should she pay the bill?"

"Maybe she's crazy about him," answered Virginia.

"It's either that or she wants to know what he knows about who killed Rosenkraatz, like everybody else." Erickson then turned his full gaze on his dining partner. "You are a smart girl, Virginia. You must have your own ideas of who wanted to do away with the Rose King."

"If I knew, I would tell the police. It would save them a long investigation."

"Takes time away from trying to figure out who killed my roses," complained Erickson.

"Forget the rose killer," suggested Virginia. "Think about being president of your country club. You know that they want you to be president."

"Are you asking me to take a presidency I don't want?"

"I wouldn't ask you to do anything you didn't want to do, but think about the prestige and what it might mean to your business."

"Here's what I think about that presidency. Let's talk about people I don't like." Erickson held up his fingers one by one. "There are three men. One, the psychiatrist who is always telling me how to improve my putting. Two, that sorehead construction man always asking me to recount my score on the 5th hole. Three, the groundskeeper who follows me around with his ground repair kit. Need I say more?"

"No, you will go your own way, no matter what," said a disgusted Virginia who changed the subject.

"You want to be a detective? You want to find the murderers of both the roses and Rosenkraatz? Is that your next move?"

"Here is what I want you to do," said E.E. "Get in touch with that Arboretum curator, what's his name. . . ."

"Bernard Crow," Virginia filled in.

"Yea, yea, yea. Anyway, talk him into giving you the phone numbers and addresses of all the volunteers and groundskeepers that were there on the day of the killings," E.E. directed.

"What are you going to do with them?" asked Virginia.

"I will invite them to a party, my treat," replied E.E.

"Why?"

"I have a reason to get these people together again," hinted Erickson.

"Please tell me what it is," whispered a curious Virginia.

"We will invite them all to my little house for cocktails, then go to the Como Park Pavilion for a box lunch and, from there, a tour of the Como Park Conservatory."

"What about the detectives? Michael Moore and Madeline Moore?"

"Invite them, too," said Erickson with a grin. "They need all the help they can get."

"I'll get all the addresses, as you say, but I don't like

the idea," said Virginia. "Do you want Bernard Crow to have someone mark the box lunches again?"

"Why not?" said Erickson shrugging his shoulders. "It will be just like a 'Thin Man' mystery when William Power gets all the suspects together."

With that final crazy idea, the two finished their meals and got up to leave the Lexington. As Virginia and E.E. Erickson began to exit, the genial host MacDuff (who did not own the Lex but acted as if he did) kissed Virginia on the forehead and shook hands with E.E.

"Thanks for coming in. The service O.K.? You don't mind my kissing your secretary, do you?" MacDuff asked E.E.

"I don't think she has cause to worry from me. Confidentially, when my wife comes in here with me, she looks forward to your unasked-for greeting," Erickson confessed.

Virginia couldn't help joining in the conversation: "Many of the girls from work come here just for the thrill of MacDuff's kiss."

"You are much too kind," gushed MacDuff.

"How come you can get away with bussing all the pretty girls," asked Erickson.

"I started it when I came out of the Marines just after World War II. No one minded then, and now they're all used to it."

"I would think it was not very sanitary," said Virginia.

Erickson and MacDuff both laughed, and then Erickson took his secretary's arm. "C'mon. We had better leave a space for MacDuff's next victim."

Crow asked Bebe after they had gotten into her red Mustang and driven a few blocks, "Did you see the couple at the far table in the restaurant, the old man and the attractive middle-aged woman?"

"You mean Mr. Erickson and his secretary, Virginia Haynes?" asked Bebe.

"I have seen them in that corner before," replied Crow.

"It's common gossip that she rarely lets him out of her sight. She clings to him like a vine," Bebe commented.

"What do you know about what's going on between them that I don't know?" inquired Crow.

"I don't know anything that you wouldn't know. You're the one who invited them to the Rosenkraatz showing."

"It's no secret that Erickson is one of our biggest donors. He practically donated the Arboretum's rose garden all by himself."

"You mean his roses were the ones killed on the day Rosenkraatz died?"

"That's right." Crow changed subjects. "Rita Rosetta knows him very well. She provides all the flowers that go to his local hotels."

Bebe brightened with this comment on Rita Rosetta.

"You mean the volunteer who asked about the rose fungus?"

"She runs the best floral shop in town," offered Crow. "You may not have noticed it during the slide show, but Rita was giving a lot of attention to the author, L.T. Bush."

"All I know about romance is that every time E.E. stops, Virginia runs into him."

"What about her and the chauffeur, what's his name? Jones?"

"That's a smoke screen."

"Where did you hear that?" Crow asked. "You don't work there, but then again, I suppose at the library you meet many people who work with E.E. Tell me, what could she possibly see in him?"

"You mean besides his millions?"

"But he's flabby, out of shape, bald and smokes cigars," said Crow.

"You sound jealous," teased Bebe.

"Of him? I think I'd turn down his money if I had to take his body."

"I hear he's trying to get rid of that old executive look," Bebe said.

"What look is that?"

"The one you just described, flabby and out of shape. That is the old executive look."

"He does have that," admitted Crow."

"I don't mean to flatter you, Bernie, but you have the new executive look."

"Oh, tell me what that is."

"You are slim and trim. You portray vitality. You look like you just stepped out of the gym. How do you keep up this new executive image, Bernard?" asked Bebe with a twinkle in her eyes.

Crow blushed.

"Oh, I've embarrassed you," said Bebe, taking one hand off the steering wheel and running it through his graying hair.

"Cut it out," Crow said, "I am not at all mad about the attention." He started to put the few strands on his head back in order. "Remember, I have to get back to the Arboretum for a meeting tonight."

"What meeting is that?" asked Bebe.

"It is not a meeting exactly. I left something there that I should have turned over to the police, but I forgot to do so."

"Is it necessary to go now?" asked Bebe. "It's such a long drive."

"Absolutely."

"What is it?"

"Another note from Rosenkraatz. He handed it to me before the lecture, and I forgot to give it to the police."

"What did it say?" asked Bebe.

"It had more information about the curses someone was putting on him."

"Of what possible use could the police find for this hex material?" asked Bebe.

"Well, for one thing they could try and find out who sent the note," offered Crow.

"I would throw it away if I were you," advised Bebe.

"No way would I throw it away," said Crow. "It might be important."

By this time, Bebe had pulled into her drive. She had very little trouble convincing Crow to wait until morning to go get his letter.

# Chapter Five

The next day, Moore and Madeline met at the Green Mill.

"I am glad you could make it today, Madeline," said Moore. "I have information I want to go over with you."

"You have something you haven't told me before?"

"On the day of the murder, Rosenkraatz had two notes in his possession. One he gave to Crow, who forgot about it until last night. The victim had received the note two days before the slide showing."

Michael then gave the new note to Madeline, and she began to read.

> Let him that is a true-born gentleman
> And stands upon the honour of his birth,
> If he suppose that I have pleaded truth,
> From off this brier pluck a white rose with me.

> A wax doll of you is burning, Rosie, when it is finished, so are you.

"What do you think of that?"

"It sounds like more voodoo to me," replied Madeline.

"How can we find out who wrote this jinx?" asked Moore.

"Why don't we just get a book of quotations and see what comes up if we look up some of the more important terms," answered Madeline.

"Like 'rose?'" asked Moore.

Madeline smiled.

The server came and Moore ordered the soup of the day; Madeline, a turkey sandwich, hold the mayo.

"Which volunteer would be most likely to dabble in voodoo?" Moore wondered aloud. "I suppose we could eliminate Rita Rosetta. I don't think a former nun would not resort to anything anti-religious."

"Don't be so sure about that," said Madeline. "Many people think there is a fine line—or no line at all—between organized religions and cults."

Moore shrugged, but seemed to understand his daughter's point of view.

"With E.E. Erickson, however, this voodoo would seem to be a foolish waste of time, I believe," said Madeline.

"You might be right there," said Moore. "It seems to me that Erickson's passion about roses is more emotional than cerebral. It's hard to believe he would donate roses to the Arboretum then kill them or kill a rose expert. What's your take on John Jones?"

"He would resort to voodoo only if it affected his golf swing, according to what I've heard about him. He also doesn't seem to have the intellectual bent to come up with something like this," said Madeline as she waved the note."

"I go along with that," said Moore as he laughed.

"Now, Virginia, Erickson's secretary, is ambitious, but she wants to make a name of herself in the business world, not the world of roses," Madeline noted.

"What do you think about L.T. Bush?" asked a still smiling Moore.

"I find him most interesting," answered Madeline.

"How do you mean that, 'interesting'?"

"He wants me to see the new floral arrangements at the Como Park Conservatory."

"I'm not so sure I like you going with that guy. For all you know he might be the killer of Rosenkraatz," said Moore.

"I don't think he is out to *kill* me," said Madeline.

"What is he after then?" Moore asked.

It was Madeline's turn to smile.

"In that case," Moore said, catching her drift, "just be very careful."

The soup and sandwich came. Moore and his daughter discussed local police politics for a while as they ate. Racial profiling was a hot topic at the state capitol. Like many other initiatives that might have developed from good intentions, the means for implementing a study and funding it properly would probably prevent a bill from passing.

When she finished her meal, Madeline left the restaurant and left her father with the bill, but she paid him back with a kiss on the cheek before her departure.

"Just be careful," Moore repeated.

Madeline met Bush at the entrance to the Conservatory on a beautiful May day.

L.T. greeted Madeline with a hearty, "It's tulip time, Madeline."

"What is that supposed to mean?"

L.T. knew right away that Madeline was not too familiar with the goings on at the Conservatory.

"May I have the pleasure of taking you through our handsome Conservatory? Typical of most local residents, you have never been here before, have you?"

"No, I haven't been here before. It is sinful, isn't it?"

"I always follow the rule of loving the sinner but hating the sin," Bush offered with a bow.

"What do you know about this Conservatory? You live just a few blocks away," asked Madeline, only slightly irritated with L.T.

"It will be my pleasure to show you around," said L.T., holding out his arm.

"Thank you ever so much," said Madeline, taking

his lead. Bush led them up the stairs and paid the fifty-cent admission fee.

"First of all, you must realize what you are being taken through. In 1974, the Como Park Conservatory was named to the National Register. That means that no one can tear it down even if a big shot like E.E. Erickson donated the money to build a new one."

Madeline noted the tone in Bush's voice and thought that perhaps Bush did not like Erickson for some reason. She filed that fact away in her memory in case it became useful later.

"Please go on with the history," said Madeline.

"In June of 1962—long before you were born, no doubt—a hail storm hit this area. Frightened people, like my sister, ran to the Conservatory for shelter. She found golf ball size hail stones crashing through the roof."

"It sounds like the Conservatory took a beating," said Madeline.

"Our wonderful City Council of 1962 came to the rescue and awarded $75,000 for repairs. So you won't have to worry if you are here in a hail storm, the roof is now fiberglass," L.T. said with a smile.

"Lead on," said Madeline.

Moore's smile turned into a evil grin. "I think it is time for me to take you, Madeline, down the Banana Walkway."

The two of them strolled around the tall tropical plants to the Avenue of Palms.

"I suppose after a while you'll try to lead me down the Primrose Path," said Madeline.

"No primrose path for us," said L.T. "We are much too serious for frivolities."

This Santa Claus-looking man's wit interested Madeline.

"I don't see any ring on your finger, Madeline. Is the field open for your affections?" asked Bush.

"I have never heard an inquiry into my affections like this before," said Madeline. "Just what are you intentions?"

Quickly L.T. replied, "For starters, I can promise you more than just a rose garden, to use the old pitch. Right here in my backyard," continued Bush with a sweep of his arm as if to suggest the Conservatory belonged to him, "I can show you tulips in the spring. At Thanksgiving, I can lead you through thousands of mums of every color. In mid-winter, my show will begin with poinsettias and after that, cyclamens, cinerarias and azaleas. No need to go south in February and March, for then we will stroll through the tropical plants. Come spring, besides the tulips bursting forth, there will be crocus, lilies, daffodils, hyacinths and pansies. In the summer, I will lead you through an exciting display of flowers and plants that are difficult to grow, such as tuberous begonias, gloxinas and fancy leaf caladiums. Need I plead my case any more?" asked L.T.

"You have told me all about flowers here, but so far

nothing of what you personally have to offer me," replied Madeline.

"I offer you a man of fortune and good will," replied L.T.

"Can you give me the kind of fortune that E.E. Erickson can offer?" asked a teasing Madeline.

"That old man!" spluttered L.T., somewhat surprised by the switch to E.E. Erickson. "Has he asked for your hand?"

"No," replied Madeline, "but I'm thinking about asking him."

With that, Bush laughed and went on with his tour. "Speaking of big shots, let me digress for a moment as to why we have this beautiful Conservatory today. At one time there was a rose garden south of the Conservatory. After that came a peony and iris garden. Then came 7,000 peonies on flower hill in the park here. Backing all these additions were the elite of the city at that time: Adolph and Otto Bremer, John A. Seegar, William Hamm and Frank B. Kellogg, just to mention a few. Kellogg was the 'trust buster' known for having won cases against Standard Oil and the Union Pacific Railroad for the government!"

"How interesting," said Madeline. She always welcomed new information about St. Paul.

During this educational lecture, L.T. and Madeline came to the goldfish pond beneath the palm trees.

The reflecting pool showed an obese, well-dressed man and a cigarette advertisement kind of woman.

"Take time to smell the flowers, Madeline," advised L.T. "We may never pass by this way again."

"That is a terrible thought, sir," said Madeline.

"Do I understand that you wish to pass this way with *me* again?" asked Bush.

"You don't mess around," said Madeline.

"Gather ye rosebuds while you may," L.T. continued.

"Am I just another bud to pluck?" Madeline teased.

"A bud or a fig, madam," replied Bush. "Remember, Aristophanes encourages us to 'Pick your figs / May his be large and hard / May hers be sweet.'"

"Yes," Madeline agreed, "but Keats reminds us, 'As though a rose should shut, and be a bud again."

"You have me there, madam, you have me there," Bush said with a laugh. "You seem to know your poetry."

"A little," said Madeline. "Try this: Truth will come to light; murder cannot be hid long."

"And who said that, pray tell?" asked L.T., turning a bit more serious.

"Who else? Shakespeare," answered Madeline. "I thought I would take this time of reflection for you to tell me who you think killed Rosenkraatz."

This abrupt change in subject startled L.T. "Is this why you agreed to take this jaunt through the Conservatory?" he asked.

"I thought you understood that?" said Madeline with a mock surprise in her voice.

"And what makes you think I would know?" continued L.T.

"You were right there, weren't you, at the time?"

"Yes, I was there all right, and I believe the sandwiches were poisoned, but not by me."

"Do you think the sandwiches were poisoned before Bernard Crow received them?" asked Madeline.

"That's a possibility," said Bush.

"So everyone at the slide show is off the hook?"

"I didn't say that. In fact, I do think that someone from the volunteer group was in on this," said L.T.

"Why would anyone want to kill a man who never did anything in his life, outside of talking about roses?"

"If you are in need of my help on this case, just say so. As a mystery writer, I'm always interested in the killing of anything," offered L.T.

"The more help we can get the better we like it," said Madeline.

"First of all, we eliminate me as a suspect. Right Madeline?"

"If you say so," Madeline replied. "But you will have to convince me of that."

"I will think about that," continued L.T.

"I would like to ask you a personal question," Madeline said.

"Go ahead."

"My father tells me that at some time in your past you committed a felony. Care to tell me about it."

"We are not through the Conservatory yet. Can't it wait until I am through with this tour?"

"Certainly it can wait," answered Madeline.

"So now, on with the tour. We shall leave the gold fish pond and the palm trees and now to my favorite corner, where the primroses grow."

They walked by a little primrose bush, hardly discernible if you were not aware of it. Then the two of them came to a statue by Alonzo Hauer called "Reclining Nude." L.T. took Madeline, pulled her close, and whispered in her ear, "See those two people?"

"You mean the nudes in the statue?"

"For heaven's sake, no. Next to the statue. It's Bernard Crow and Bebe Daniels."

"Bernard Crow, the Curator?" Madeline asked. "Isn't that interesting."

"I don't think we should break into their little private time. I guess I'll have to find another place to continue wooing you, my dear Madeline. I was just about to show you the Japanese Tea Garden. We can say 'Hello' on our way out," said Bush as he continued with his tour. "The Japanese Garden was dedicated in 1979 and then rededicated in 1992. Most people don't know that this Garden was designed by a Nagasaki landscape gardener, Masami Matsuda. It is a symbol of the relationship between St. Paul and her sister city, Nagasaki, Japan."

As before, Madeline was impressed with L.T.'s knowledge of varied subjects.

"Let me tell you all about the bonsai exhibit that we have here at the Conservatory," continued Bush.

"Please do."

"First of all, I don't like where the management put this exhibit," he said.

"Why not?"

"You have to go through the gift shop to see it; that is why." After he finished complaining about that fact, Bush went on to tell Madeline that Bonsai is a specialized art form using living plant materials as a sculpture medium. Virtually any species of tree or woody shrub can be used to create a bonsai.

A bonsai artist, he continued, does not attempt to produce a scale model of life-size counterpart, but rather creates a work of art which reflects and amplifies such natural forms. Bonsai are not houseplants. They spend the majority of their lives outdoors. They require a winter dormant period just as other trees do and, if permitted, will follow the cycle of the seasons losing their leaves in the fall and renewing them again in the springtime. They continue to grow, but their growth is carefully planned. They are kept small by a process of pruning and pinching new needles, leaves and roots. The result is a living reflection of nature.

"I am changing the subject again," said Madeline after Bush's lengthy bonsai lecture, "but what do you think that Bebe Daniels and Bernard Crow have in common?" asked Madeline.

"Appetite," said Bush.

"Look," whispered Madeline. "They don't want us to see them. They are moving away."

"The guilty flee when no man pursueth," quoted Bush. "As I remember the meeting with the slide king, Rosenkraatz, it was Crow and Bebe who gave out the sandwiches."

"Then you surmise that they joined together for some reason to do away with Rosenkraatz?" asked Madeline.

"You are the detective, What is your thinking?"

"I am looking for a motive," replied Madeline.

"Let me touch on a few things I know about this Bebe Daniels," offered L.T. Bush, "right after we find a place to sit down.

"Where do you suggest we go?"

"The best place to go is where the tulips are in bloom: the sunken garden. This is the place where there is a constant change of floral displays, and right now it is tulip time!"

So the two passed through the Fern Room with its mosses and ivies that climb over the rocks lining multi-leveled paths and found a seat right in the middle of all the tulips.

"This doesn't seem like the right place to discuss murder," said Madeline.

"I am sure I could think of many other things to discuss, Miss Moore," said Bush.

"I'm sure you could," said Madeline. "But let's get back to what you know about Bebe."

Bush sighed. "Let me tell you what I find interesting about Bebe Daniels. She made it clear to all of us at Rosenkraatz's slide show that she was named for the movie star who was her father's idol. She also told the rest of the volunteers that if they wanted to really find out something about roses that to just drop by the library. By that she implied that *she* could tell them a lot more than Rosenkraatz could."

Madeline nodded.

"Now," continued L.T., "let's review the facts of the mystery. Mr. Crow gave the sandwiches to Bebe and told her to mark each one as to who gets what. Then she left the room and took all the sandwiches with her for marking. And mind you, she was in the room alone for some time marking the sandwiches."

"What would be her motive in poisoning Rosenkraatz?"

"Jealousy."

"Professional jealousy?" Madeline asked. "Or another kind?"

"I suspect a little of both."

"What do you mean by that?"

"If you want any further information, you'll have to give me something in return."

"And what would that be?" asked Madeline.

"I'd like to continue to see you, but under better, more romantic conditions."

Although she didn't want to, Madeline blushed.

"That would be unprofessional," Madeline finally said.

"Perhaps we could make it a more public forum. I am a gourmet cook besides my many other talents. The end of next week, Saturday to be exact, I am going to invite all the volunteers to my abode for an exciting evening, and a meal you could only get at the Ritz in Paris or the Lexington in St. Paul."

Madeline told him she would make an appearance if possible. Then she excused herself, telling Bush she had another engagement.

After she left, she realized he had not told her anything she didn't know about Bebe, and he had not told her about his arrest record.

# Chapter Six

She called her father as soon as she got back to the office.

"What kept you?" Moore asked.

"I just wasted a couple hours at the Como Park Conservatory," said Madeline.

"What did you discover that might be of interest?" Moore asked

"Not much, except for the fact that Bebe Daniels and Bernard Crow were anxious not to let me see them together."

"They were there, too?" her father asked.

"Yes," said Madeline. "Quite a coincidence and perhaps an embarrassment for them. What did you find out?"

"Bush did time for embezzlement."

"You mean someone was dumb enough to let him take care of their money or property?"

"Exactly," said Michael.

"Give me the details. I want to know all about it," said Madeline.

"Apparently he traveled to the Rose Bowl Parade without telling anyone of his whereabouts. He missed a committee meeting for a local private school which he served as treasurer. A member of the school board who didn't like L.T. got suspicious. An audit found $3,000 missing from the pop fund."

"The what?" said Madeline.

"The pop fund. Schools sell exclusive rights to certain brands of pop. It's quite lucrative. Anyway, on L.T.'s return from the Rose Bowl trip, he was arrested and booked on embezzlement, and that is when he was fingerprinted. He spent a year in the work house and paid a fine."

"He keeps telling me that he's independently wealthy."

"Who knows why he did it," said Moore. "Maybe he's not telling you the truth about his financial situation, or maybe he thought he could get away with it."

"But going from embezzlement to murder is a stretch," said Madeline.

"I suppose, but it is still interesting that his fingerprints were on that can of Roundup," observed Moore.

"Did it occur that he might have bought that can for someone else?" said Madeline.

"That did occur to me."

"Are you getting closer to the solution?"

"I think I can solve both the rose killing and what happened to Rosenkraatz in short order," offered Moore.

"Tell me more, Captain Moore," said Madeline.

"Let me tell you what I have found since we talked last, and of course, let me know what you think to make sure I am not wrong. You know I obtained a complete list of all the volunteers that were at Ralph Rosenkraatz's slide showing. I gave you a copy of the list. Right?" began Moore.

"Right," said Madeline.

"Let's begin with Bernard Crow," continued Moore. "I got hold of his high school year book. Under Crow's picture was the following: 'Class egghead . . . botanist . . . best friend . . . Rosie.' Here in the same book was Rosenkraatz and under his name: 'Rosie . . . botanist . . . track star . . . Golden Gloves . . . ambition: travel the world.'"

Madeline broke in on this high school sketch of Crow, "What was that connection between Crow and Rosie? I thought Crow said he didn't meet Rosenkraatz until his sister's wedding."

"It appears that he was lying."

"Why would he do that?" asked Madeline.

"You tell me."

"I suppose he didn't want us to know something."

"Like the fact that Rosenkraatz ran off with his kid sister and the fact that they lived together a long time before they were married. Maybe Crow introduced the two of them and felt responsible. The neighbors heard Crow threaten several times that if Rosie didn't marry his sister, he would kill him."

"But they did get married," Madeline interjected. "And they seem to be best friends again."

"Seem to be," said Moore. "After Bernard Crow, I investigated Rita Rosetta. I wanted to find out why she left the convent and started her own floral shop. The other nuns can be pretty tight lipped.

"Are you telling me you went to the Sisters of Carondolett?" asked Madeline.

"Where else could I find out?" asked Moore.

"The Mother Superior, no doubt, put out the welcome mat for you," Madeline sarcastically said.

"She was most helpful."

"What did she tell you about Rita?"

"First of all, I asked her why Rita became a nun."

"Why would she tell you?"

"Have you forgotten I have two aunts in the same order. After I reminded the Mother Superior of that fact she felt free to talk to me."

"What did she tell you about Rita Rosetta?"

"She went into the sisterhood the same time as her fraternal twin sister did."

"She had a twin sister?"

"Apparently, and just as boys at the time wanted to become firemen or policemen, Rita and her sister wanted to become nuns. The convent welcomed them with open arms and rosaries. Rita and her sister came from a respectable family. Rita's sister made it only a year and then became homesick. She cried all the way back to her house. This didn't go too well with Rita, but she stayed on for a while longer."

"Remarkable," said Madeline, "that the Mother Superior would tell you all this."

"I have a natural talent for listening," bragged Moore. "Sister went on to tell me just what happened to Rita, and why she left the Convent. One year after her sister left, she came driving up to see Rita in a brand new Mustang. Rita cried when her twin left in the fancy car. Mother Superior said she came to them in the first place because her two aunts from Saint Peter wanted her to be a nun, something they had wanted to be but didn't because of family obligations, if you get my drift. In any event, the chastity part got to the aunts. It was apparently the vow of poverty that got to Rita. She wanted a nice car, too. The Mother Superior also confided in me that she believed the vow of poverty to be the toughest one to make in this materialistic world."

"Where is the twin sister today?" asked Madeline.

"She ran away from home and headed west with a slapping guitar player from Shakopee."

"I suppose you think the twin sister is back in town with a new name and her Mustang?" asked Madeline.

"That's possible," said Moore, "but even if Bebe Daniels is the long-lost sister, I'm not sure that that gets us any closer to the killer."

"This case just keeps getting more curious," said Madeline.

"It certainly does," said Moore, looking at his watch. "Look, I have to go to a meeting, but let's meet tomorrow for lunch and we can go over some more of this case."

"Your turn to buy?"

"I thought I paid last time."

"Dad, you always say that."

"O.K. My turn. But I'm writing it down this time." Both father and daughter had a good laugh about that.

# Chapter Seven

Michael turned out to be busy the next day, so he and Madeline didn't get a chance to meet until the night of Bush's party. They drove separately and managed to talk a bit in the back yard after what Madeline had assured Bush was certainly as delightful as anything the Ritz had to offer, even though she had never been there herself.

"I found out something interesting about Rita," started Moore. "L.T. called to ask if I could pick up Rita and bring her along, too, since her car was getting repaired. So I called Rita. She was most pleasantly surprised, not only by the invitation she had received, but also by my call. On the way to Bush's house, she confided in me that she had great interest in L.T. Bush. He reminded her of her father, who also was built like a jovial Santa Claus. She also told me she was taking cooking lessons so she could some day cook for Bush."

"I wonder if L.T. knows about this silent admirer," interjected Madeline. "His attempts to seduce me would at the very least suggest he didn't care."

"Or at least wanted you to think that, perhaps to throw you off track," offered Moore. "I asked Rita what she thought about the murder. She said she didn't do it, of course, and that she couldn't imagine such a wonderful man as L.T. Bush could do such a thing either."

At that point Bush came outside into the cool May night.

"How do you like my gardens, Mr. Moore?" Bush asked.

"I don't know much about gardening," Moore admitted, "but it's very pleasant here."

"Thank you," said Bush, "now if you'll excuse me, I have to see to my other guests."

Virginia came out next. During her conversation with the Moores, she let slip that she had lived near Como Park as a teenager and had gone to a nearby parochial school. "I had high marks," she said, "so I used my knowledge to become a nurse, but I didn't like the work so I quit to go to work for Erickson," she said.

"We're you his personal secretary from the beginning?" asked Madeline.

"No," Virginia answered. "I first worked as a file

clerk, then I was put in charge of the stenographic department and from there I became E.E.'s personal assistant. I have been in that position for fifteen years."

"How do you like your job?" asked Moore.

"Is this an interrogation?"

"No, not really. I'm just curious," Moore replied.

"Actually, the only thing I dislike about my job is dealing with roses all the time."

A phone rang, and Moore noticed her digging into an oversized purse for her cell phone. She answered it and then said to the Moores. "Excuse me. I'm afraid some business has come up that I have to take care of."

She went back into the house.

"Did you notice that purse?" asked Moore of his daughter.

"Sure did," said Madeline. "Big enough to carry a can of Roundup."

"If anyone at the lecture had made arrangements to kill E.E.'s roses at the Arboretum, it most likely was Virginia,"

"Perhaps it was her way of getting back at E.E. for the little attention he gave her romantic advances," said Madeline.

"How do you know about that?" asked Moore, surprised at his daughter's revelation.

"I did get a couple good things from our dear friend Mr. Bush these past couple days. "And that brings me to the killer can found with L.T. Bush's fingerprints on it. I am convinced without a doubt that Virginia talked L.T. into getting that can of Roundup for her."

"So now all we have to do is find out how Virginia ditched Jones while she poisoned the plants."

"Maybe he helped her," offered Madeline.

"You could be right," said Moore. "When Virginia said 'Jump!' Jones asked 'How high?'"

"I'll have to corner Jones tonight," said Madeline, "and see if he can shed any light on Virginia's whereabouts the day of the murder."

"Next," said Moore, "your information about Bebe and Bernard in the Conservatory got me thinking, so I figured I'd ask her about it."

"What did she say?" asked Madeline.

Moore explained that Bebe called Bernard a "double crossing cheater" and had known him before the slide showing.

"She told me she had loved him once," Moore continued, "and then implied that something was going on between Bernard and Rosenkraatz."

"But all our other information tends to indicate that Bernard had reason for disliking Rosenkraatz," said a puzzled Madeline.

"I know," said Moore. "But that's not the end of it. She also told me she thought the killer got the wrong person."

"Whom did she think the killer was really after?" asked Madeline. "Did she say?"

"Your friend, L.T. Bush."

Madeline was silent for a while, so Moore continued. "I confirmed that she was the one who gave the lethal sandwich to Rosenkraatz. She admitted that freely, but she denied that either she or Crow had tampered with the boxes."

"Did her facial expressions give anything away?" Madeline asked.

"Her infatuation with Crow interests me," she replied. "She could have killed Rosenkraatz for stealing Crow away from her."

"That's certainly a possibility," admitted Moore, "but I still think L.T. Bush also knows more than he's willing to divulge."

"You have something on him?"

"You be the judge of what I am going to tell you about this Lothario," answered Moore. "Once I got him on the topic, he told me sales of his book *The Rose in Her Hair* are now taking off since the killing of Rosenkraatz."

"Where did the newspaper people get all the information about who was at the scene of the murder?" asked Madeline.

"Crow gave it to them," Moore responded.

At that point, Bush came back to the gardens. "Ah, the two Moores," he said with a laugh. "I see you're still trying to fit all the pieces of the puzzle together."

When neither the father nor daughter spoke, he continued. "You couldn't possibly suspect me of killing Rosenkraatz could you?"

"You were there at the scene of the crime when someone did away with Rosenkraatz and also killed the roses," said Madeline.

"I'm interested in roses and the planting of them," stated L.T. Bush, "so naturally I was there. I admire have always admired the Como Conservatory exhibits and because of this I took up digging in dirt and planting roses myself. Dirty hands are the best mental therapy of all. My philosophy is be calm, be serene, be dirty. When you have worries about life, your children, finances, or whatever, get your hands dirty in the soil.

"I'm sure I read somewhere that a person's blood pressure drops dramatically when fooling around in the dirt. I follow my own advice and came that day to hear more about roses. Now you know my secrets, Captain Moore. I was at the slide show just looking for more ways to dig in the dirt."

"So what dirt did you dig up on Rosenkraatz?" asked Moore.

"Nobody appeared to have a strong motive for killing him. For example, Wendall Holmes. Did you know he was a letter carrier? He simply looks into the paper to find unusual things to do on his day off. Since he likes songs about roses, he decided to go to a lecture about roses. It's hard to believe that he would commit murder.

Now, concerning the rose killing: we have only a case of vandalism. It takes no great intellect to reach the conclusion that Virginia was behind the Roundup dustoff. When she and this playboy Jones came back from their intermission, she cried, to the amazement of all, that someone had killed the roses. She obviously was, and is, in love with E.E., and this act of hers was the equivalent of slapping him in the face for his lack of attention to her."

"Very enlightening," agreed Moore. "But why were your fingerprints on the Roundup can, and why would Jones go along with Virginia?"

Bush raised his eyebrows. "I can tell you the answer to both questions. When we came into the room for the lecture, I tripped over a large bag and something fell out. That something was a can of Roundup. Naturally, I put it back into the bag. It turns out that bag was Virginia's purse."

Both Moore and his daughter were excited by this new piece of information, but both tried to keep their feelings from being mirrored on their faces.

"As for Jones," Bush continued. "She either ditched him long enough to put the poison on the plants, or she could have told him it was fertilizer. How would he know?"

"Supposition is one thing; proof is another," said Moore. "Will you testify that Virginia had the Roundup can?"

L.T. laughed. "You have to charge them first."

"Let's get to the important things," said Moore. "Who killed Rosenkraatz?"

"As far as I have determined, Bebe and Crow once

were lovers, which is the reason Crow had Bebe help him with the box lunches."

"You mean he thought he could trust her with the assignment?" asked Moore.

"Implicitly. Crow didn't realize that Bebe was smoldering from their breakup."

"Your conclusion is that Bebe killed Rosenkraatz because he left her for another?" asked Madeline.

"Precisely what I think," said Bush. "Look at all the witnesses who saw Bebe give the sandwiches to Rosenkraatz. Need I say more?"

"But just because she marked the boxes doesn't mean she poisoned the sandwich. Did you notice any of the boxes having been tampered with when they were handed out? And did you see Bebe carry anything into the room where she put labels on the sandwiches?"

Bush admitted that he could remember nothing of the sort, but told Moore to confront both Bebe and Virginia.

The Moores said goodbye to him at that point, and left after thanking him for a wonderful evening.

L.T. was dismayed at Madeline's sudden departure, but he soon got over it.

# Chapter Eight

Moore and Madeline met the next day for lunch at the St. Clair Broiler.

"Are you saying you are finished with the case?" she asked her father.

"I think we know who did it; we just need to find the proof."

"Are you telling me you're willing to accept what L.T. Bush has laid out as the scenario for the murders?"

"Certainly . . . only because I think he is right," said Moore in between spoonfuls of the cream of potato soup.

"In any event, we will have a chance to see all the suspects at E.E.'s party at his country club for all the volunteers at the end of next week. I have my invitation and I am sure you have yours?"

"Yes, I'll be there," said Madeline.

"It sounds very exciting, an exact duplicate of a famous dinner at the Ritz in Paris."

Madeline added, "It is the only invitation for dinner I have ever received that listed the menu on the invitation."

Madeline nibbled at her sandwich. Moore could tell something was wrong. "What's bugging you?" he asked.

"First of all, you eliminated the only person of all the volunteers with a criminal record, L.T. Bush. Why?" inquired Madeline.

"I think he loves roses too much to kill them, and if he had carried an Roundup can into the lecture, someone would have spotted him. Whereas his story about the can being in Virginia's large bag makes perfect sense.

Madeline nodded. "But you also overlooked the hummer, Wendall Holmes. Why? As a member of the Sherlock Club, he possesses the most knowledge about crime of all the volunteers. Members of that group study crime and criminal behavior as a hobby. Maybe he had in mind the perfect crime."

"Like killing the wrong victim accidentally? That doesn't make sense," said Moore.

"I guess you're right," said Madeline. "But what about the tycoon, E.E. Erickson? Is he off your hook?"

"He has no motive for killing anybody. He has what all of us desire: wealth, prestige, reputation. As far as I can tell, he has no connection to Rosenkraatz whatsoever. E.E. is a happily married Presbyterian," Moore summarized.

"Why Presbyterian?" Madeline asked.

"Remember, Madeline, their bible is the *Wall Street Journal*."

"That is a terrible thing to say, Father," Madeline scolded. "Tell me the real reason you figure E.E. is a Presbyterian?"

"Very simple," Moore happily responded. "The doorman at his country club told me that on Sunday mornings he always tells his chauffeur, Jones, to go pick up his wife at the House of Hope."

"Do you know how he made all that money?" asked Madeline.

"He started as a bell-hop and worked his way up. A typical rags to riches story in the tradition of Horatio Alger. Before E.E. took over the hotels, the former owner of the chain sent him to the Siberia of the chain, both literally and figuratively."

"Where is that?" asked Madeline.

"Fargo."

They both got a laugh out of that.

"And how did E.E. do in Fargo?"

"An incredible performance. This weakest link in the chain of twelve hotels took off. The owner brought E.E. down to Minneapolis, and from there the rest is history. The flagship hotel in Minneapolis became an outstanding hotel, and soon its new manager,

E.E., became vice president and then, shortly, the owner."

"You found all this out from the doorman at the country club?" questioned Madeline.

"Well, not all of it," admitted Moore modestly.

"And the whole story came from where?"

"You might be surprised to hear I found this out from one of the members of the volunteers, Wendall Holmes."

"You have seen Holmes?"

"Of course," answered Moore, "I leave no stone unturned in my investigation. Holmes, as you know, is a member of the Sherlock Holmes Literary Society, as is L.T. Bush. Holmes even took a course in wood carving because slivers from the ladder led to the arrest of Hauptman in the Lindbergh case. He figured he wanted to know as much about wood as possible just in case another crime revolved around a wooden clue."

"That's interesting, but what does he know about E.E.?" asked Madeline.

"He knew," said Moore, "that wood carving was one of E.E.'s hobbies. He learned that E.E. preferred basswood for his carvings because it works well and is found in great supply in Minnesota."

"Is that all you found out? That seems like a waste of time."

"Perhaps, but people who share hobbies are more willing to tell about themselves to a buddy with the same hobby. Don't you think?" asked Moore.

"Did you find out if E.E. had any enemies? You know the rich always do. Either they clawed their way to the top, or there is always some crackpot around who thinks he's Jesse James."

"I am sure he must have some enemies. So you still think the killer did in the wrong person?" asked Moore.

"No harm in thinking that, is there?" replied Madeline with a smile. "But you didn't really answer my question. Did you find out anything else?"

"That is all I got out of Holmes," confessed Moore. "But I hope we will be able to wrap this up at Erickson's party."

# Chapter Nine

E.E.'s Invitation for his Ritz party read:

**WE'RE PUTTIN' ON THE RITZ**

Come all rose lovers to a RITZ party at my Country Club!

*Date:* September 5
*Time:* 8 p.m.
*Dress:* Casual
*Menu:* (1) Champagne served with a rose
       (2) Bowls of olives soaked in cognac
       (3) Water with raspberries
       (4) Medallions of lamb encrusted in bread and black
       (5) Chestnut parfait

If you can't digest, we will serve you Melba toast and Peach Melba named after French soprano Dame Nellie Melba.

## Please RSVP

All of the volunteers who were present when Rosenkraatz was poisoned agreed to attend, although the first people to accept were Michael and Madeline Moore.

The night of the party came. Moore inquired as he arrived at the club if anyone was missing?

Crow responded, "Every volunteer I know of who was at the Rosenkraatz slide showing is here."

E.E. had Virginia arrange to have the dinner in a special room set aside for important occasions. Wide-eyed club friends of E.E. stared at this strange array of guests. Certainly none of the guests looked like typical members.

Virginia, acting as the hostess, directed the volunteers to the room for the Ritz feast. They easily found their names on little cards around the table. Per E.E.'s instructions, Madeline sat on his right and Moore sat at his left. This placement of the two detectives gave the appearances that E.E. desired police protection. Madeline made a beautiful addition to the head table with her brilliant red hair and yellow strapless dress.

In counter-clockwise order from Madeline sat the

following: L.T. Bush, Rita Rosetta, Virginia Haynes, John Jones, Bebe Daniels, Bernard Crow, and Wendall Holmes—a motley crew indeed for the swank country club.

When they were all seated, E.E. took his sterling silver butter knife and gently tapped the crystal drinking glass for attention. E.E. opened the dinner with a toast, "Here is a toast to roses, to the flower we all love so well."

The servers gave a rose to each of the ladies and poured champagne into their wineglasses.

"I'll go along with that toast," cried L.T. Bush.

"Me, too," agreed Holmes.

"Anybody want a Louis XIII?" asked E.E.

"What in the world is that?" asked Bebe Daniels.

"It is the Club Special, although in this case 'special' does not mean a lower cost; the drink is $66."

"Are you paying for them?" asked Virginia.

"If anyone can hold that drink, Virginia, just put it on my tab, but be sure to keep an eye on anyone who dares take that fifty-year-old cognac," cautioned E.E.

"That drink is older than I am," said Rita Rosetta.

If anyone in the room had the capacity to hold a Louis XIII it would be L.T. Bush. He had the size to digest it slowly; whereas a drink that powerful would go through a slim fifty year old such as Rita at sixty miles per hour.

"I'll take one," said L.T. with a smile. He managed to gulp it in two seconds.

"I'll have one myself," said E.E. "So none for you, John, since after this I really will need a ride home."

After no one else ordered a Louis XIII, E.E. began to explain why he invited so many to his club.

"Some of you," began E.E., "might wonder why I am gathering all you volunteers after the horrible experience we had the last time we all met."

Virginia was the only one who nodded her head. Bebe Daniels, who had tried to dress like her namesake, didn't acknowledge Erickson because she was too busy casting adoring eyes at Bernard Crow. Crow didn't like her attention and seemed embarrassed by it. Still, he whispered to Bebe: "Did you notice when E.E. Erickson lifted his glass for a toast that he carries a pistol in his belt?"

"No," said Bebe, who diverted her attention from Crow long enough to look at Erickson.

"Rumor has it," continued Crow, "that he has a fear that some day he will be kidnapped."

"Are you making that up?" asked Bebe.

"How could I make up what I saw?"

E.E. noticed the two whispering to each other and cleared his voice loudly. "May I have your attention, please." This embarrassed both Crow and Bebe, and they stopped whispering at once. "You will never find a meal like this except in the Ritz in Paris," Erickson continued. "I thought, how could anyone skip an invitation to a meal similar to world class restaurant like the Ritz? And not one of you disappointed me. Thank you one and all for coming." Erickson made a few more comments about how the rose world would sorely miss Rosenkraatz but that they all must go on with their lives.

"Some of you have already been contacted by Detective Michael Moore of the local police station and others may have been contacted by his daughter, Detective Madeline Moore," Erickson went on.

No one reacted to the introductions except Virginia, who gave a slight smirk.

"These two very clever officers have come up with some astounding findings, not only about who killed my roses, but who did away with Ralph Rosenkraatz. But finish your meal first before we come to these amazing discoveries," Erickson finished.

It was Virginia's idea to sit herself next to John Jones. She felt he didn't fit in with anybody else in the group. After all, they were simply second-rate writers, flower shop owners, postal workers, detectives, and other people who would never understand what it meant to be in the social register. At least with Jones, she could carry on a conversation about the Twins and Vikings if she got really bored.

Virginia, who usually wore a suit to work, had put on a backless, form-hugging dress that accentuated her best assets. Everyone at the table had looked at her at least once and had made some mental observation, positive or negative.

John Jones, dressed in a gabardine suit and two-tone

shoes, asked Virginia, "Do you have any idea why he is having this gathering? Of all people, he must have told you why."

"I don't know anymore about this gathering than you do," replied Virginia.

"Very peculiar to me that all these people are suspects in the murder of Rosenkraatz," said Jones.

"Brilliant observation, Johnny," Virginia teased.

Jones was flabbergasted because Virginia had never called him 'Johnny' before.

Wendall Holmes, seated next to Moore, asked the detective, "It seems you are hot on the trail of whoever killed Rosenkraatz. Do you plan to announce the killer here tonight?"

Moore took his time answering as he slurped away at his French onion soup. "You will know soon enough," he said.

"I can hardly wait," Holmes countered.

When the meal was over and dessert was passed around, E.E. nodded at Moore, who stood up. Before Moore started to speak, John Jones stood, but Virginia pulled him back down to his seat.

"Please, don't go anywhere," Moore said to Jones. "This party is not over just yet."

"It is for me," whispered Jones to Virginia.

Moore continued, "Don't become alarmed, any of you, by the appearance of my daughter and myself."

L.T. Bush interrupted Moore with this toast:

"Here's to Louis the XIII. *Vive La France*. I'll have another one."

E.E. smiled, even though another $66 would be added to his tab. Rita Rosetta tried to quiet L.T. down, but he just scolded, "Don't bother me, little girl."

Rita almost cried over this admonition. She didn't like to be called "little" any better than Madeline did. Moore sensed that trouble lay ahead if no one could contain the loud-mouthed L.T. Bush, but he knew that he and Madeline could handle anything that might arise.

Moore then said, "Of great concern to Mr. E.E. Erickson was the killing of his special mound of roses that he pays for at the Arboretum. My daughter, Madeline, and I worked diligently to find out who committed this act of vandalism. We still don't know who did it, but we do know who didn't do it."

L.T. yelled out, "Tell them who I think did it, Moore."

"L.T., you are a guest, not a detective," cautioned Erickson. "Please be still for now. You and the other guests need to hold your comments until Captain Moore is finished."

Moore continued, "Madeline found a can of Roundup near the rose mound in her initial search for anything that might have killed the roses. We have determined since then that for Roundup to kill roses, it needs at least 12 to 24 hours to do its dirty work. So any suspicion that Virginia and Jones did the job is out the window. They are not suspects now as the rose killers. Virginia and John may rest easy."

Virginia was irate: "Who ever said we *were* suspects of the rose killings?"

"Our loudmouth friend, L.T. Bush, I bet," said Jones.

"That's right," said Moore. "Bush indicated he saw a can of Roundup in your bag when you came to the lecture. But whoever killed the roses must have done so the night *before* the Rosenkraatz slide showing, so it didn't make any sense for the killer to carry around the can for an entire day."

E.E. could no longer be quiet and jumped to his feet, "So who did kill my roses?"

Madeline rose to try to calm E.E. down. "Mr. Erickson, if you will bear with us a while longer, we think we can tell you exactly who killed the roses and who did away with Ralph Rosenkraatz."

Wendall Holmes jumped up from his chair and demanded, "What kind of a celebration is this?"

Moore stopped him by saying, "This is a celebration for all the lovers of roses."

"It looks to me like the end of a William Powell 'Thin Man' movie," said Holmes. "You have all the suspects in the room under the pretense of a party at the Ritz."

Bebe Daniels shouted her support for Holmes: "You got that right, Mr. Holmes."

Virginia chimed in with, "You all are not very grateful. How many people do you know have ever had a chance to eat at the Ritz in Paris and have the meal we are getting here tonight?"

L.T. Bush spoke up, "I'd rather have the meal that Moore and I had at my house, the good old American meal of ham, potatoes, gravy and peas, plus apple pie for dessert."

E.E. obviously didn't like this renegade in his Ritz-style meal and said so. "It looks to me like you will eat anything served you."

L.T. tried to rise to his feet, but couldn't manage. Before Erickson could go on, Madeline interrupted. "I shall go on with our findings. I went to the library, but I made sure our rose friend," at this point she pointed toward Bebe, "was not on duty so I could I talked to another librarian. From him, I discovered that a man had been in the library asking about information on hexes. I asked her to describe him for me. She said he was very handsome and all the time he was there, he kept humming the tune, 'The Last Rose of Summer.'

"The librarian asked him why he was interested in hexes, and he replied, 'None of your business.'"

Bebe Daniels exclaimed, "I know who the hummer is. He comes to the library often. It is that man right there." With this, she pointed at Wendall Holmes.

Holmes rose in his defense. "I go to the library for many reasons, not just to check on hexes, which are of interest to many members of the Sherlock Holmes Society."

Madeline directed her next question to Holmes: "So what were you there for?"

Holmes replied: "I had an assignment from the Sherlock Holmes Society to find out all I could about the number thirteen."

"And what did you find?" asked E.E.

"Oh, lots of things, For example, take a dollar bill from your pocket if you want to play along. If you count the steps of the pyramid, you will find there are exactly thirteen. The motto above the pyramid 'Annuit coeptis' has thirteen letters. The bald eagle on the right side has a ribbon in its beak that bears the motto 'E pluribus unum,' which also has thirteen letters. Over the eagle's head are thirteen stars. There are thirteen stripes on the shield. The eagle's left holds thirteen war arrows and its right talon holds an olive branch of peace with thirteen leaves...."

"I've had enough of this nonsense," said Madeline. "You can see Mr. Holmes is not only interested in numerology, but also interested in changing the subject."

Before Madeline could go on, Rita Rosetta interrupted, "Mr. Holmes, you have not told us just when and why the number thirteen is a jinx."

Rita then explained her interpretation of the number thirteen. "Of course I know all about the number thirteen and when it got its jinx. The fact is that when the thirteen people attended the Last Supper of Christ, the betrayal and death of Christ followed. This happening occurred when the twelve apostles and Christ came to a total of thirteen. That is how it got its evil reputation. It was thought to be very unlucky for thirteen people to sit down to a table. One was sure to die and suffer some damage and misfortune before the year was out. I believe that the number thirteen was drawn directly from the role of Christ and his apostles."

With this long explanation, Rita sat down with a sweet smile of contentment that showed she had had her say.

"Very good, Rita," said Holmes. "But let me carry this a little further. The uneasiness about thirteen is older than Christianity, for even the Romans associated thirteen with death and misfortune. The root reason may be that thirteen is one more than twelve, which is the number of completeness, the whole year consisting of twelve months, the whole day consisting of twice twelve hours. And so thirteen has the connotation of dangerously exceeding proper limits, of going beyond a natural cycle or starting on a new and uncertain course."

John Jones jumped in. "Thirteen is a lucky number for me, E.E. Remember when I got a hole in one on the 265-yard thirteenth hole on a Friday the thirteenth?"

"You had plenty of wind at your back on that day, John. I remember it well," said E.E.

Bebe Daniels was not going to let this go by

without telling everyone about what she thought about the luck or the bad luck of the number thirteen. "I was born on the thirteenth, on a Friday, the thirteenth child born that day at my hospital. My sister found the Winter Carnival Treasure Chest on the thirteenth clue one year. That was worth thousands of dollars."

"That's enough of this nonsense about thirteen," said Erickson. "Would you please continue Miss Moore?"

Madeline smiled and then started up again. "The librarian also told me at the time Holmes was there, he wanted to see a poem written by the poetess Christina Rossetti, no relation to Rita, called 'Sister Helen.'"

There was a buzz among the remainder of the volunteers.

"And that poem was quoted in a letter written to Rosenkraatz threatening his life," added Moore.

The ever-nosy L.T. asked, "What is all this about 'Sister Helen'?"

Madeline said, "I don't think we have to give all secrets to Mr. L.T. Bush."

"Why not?" demanded L.T.

"Don't you forget, Mr. Bush, you were a witness to all that took place when Mr. Rosenkraatz's death occurred, and that means you yourself could be involved in his death," said Moore. "And *we*," at this Moore pointed to his daughter, "will certainly not forget that you lied about the Roundup can." Moore was very irritated with L.T. Bush's attempt to sidetrack the investigation.

Thoroughly exasperated, E.E. said, "Let us go on with the killers, Madeline. Who killed my roses?"

Right then in came a server with the name Amy on her nametag to ask if anyone would like an after dinner aperitif.

"Just like at the Ritz," said E.E.

"Yes sir," Amy replied.

"By the way, Amy," slurred an obviously intoxicated L.T. Bush, "I was very impressed by the dessert from the Ritz. But why wasn't there any ice cream?"

Amy replied, "You don't get ice cream at the Ritz with chestnut parfait."

"When was the last time *you* were at the Ritz?" L.T. asked.

Hurt by the tone of his voice, Amy left the room without taking any orders.

Madeline stood up and took E.E.'s fork and hit the crystal glass. "May I have your attention, please?"

"Why?" asked L.T.

"I am going to pronounce all of you not guilty of killing the roses, except one, and that one knows who he is."

"Did you ever think I would kill roses?" asked Rita.

"We suspected everyone," said Moore.

"Why would I cut out my business from Mr. Erickson? He buys his roses from me. I would have no reason to pick on his roses."

"Are you going to question everyone here about the damned dead roses?" stormed L.T.

"You bet I am, right up until someone stands up and says 'I did it,'" Madeline said.

"Isn't that against the law?" asked Jones. "Where did you come up with this idea of cat and mouse?"

"Yea," said Bush, "what gives?"

"You might, Mr. L.T. Bush," said Madeline.

"Don't be cute with me, little girl. I have already told that gentleman next to Mr. Erickson, Detective Michael Moore, just who killed the rose bushes."

E.E. turned to Moore and asked: "You know who did this dastardly act?"

"L.T. Bush had me thinking for a while that a certain someone did it. But evidently my daughter thinks otherwise, right Madeline?" asked Moore, turning to his daughter.

Madeline responded, "Let us hear from L.T. Bush what he told you concerning who did the deed."

"He asked me to simply find out who left the lecture while Rosenkraatz showed his slides," Moore said.

Wendall Holmes eagerly jumped in. "We all know who left," he said and pointed toward Virginia and Jones. "Those two lovers left and came back with the discovery that someone had killed the rose bushes."

Virginia jumped to her feet, "We discovered who did the act and reported it."

"So you say," remarked L.T.

"And what do you mean by that sarcastic remark?" Jones said to L.T. in a threatening manner.

L.T. was quick to answer. "I saw your girlfriend there dump a can into the wastebasket when you returned. I picked up the can afterwards and noticed it was a can of Roundup. Explain that."

"You're lying," said Virginia. "Captain Moore has already indicated that Roundup takes at least twelve hours to work. Why would I bring the can back after twelve hours?"

"That is a good point," declared E.E., coming to her defense.

"I would never even think of that horrible act of vandalism," protested Virginia.

"So you say," L.T. responded. "Maybe you killed them the day before and forgot the can. When you went to the Arboretum that day, you found the can, put it in your purse, and then waited for a time to throw it away.

Rita broke in with, "What makes you think you know what happened, Mr. Bush?"

"Keep this little girl out of it," scolded L.T., "and bring us more drinks and curry powder."

"What is that all about?" asked E.E.

"Allow me to tell you, Mr. Erickson. Look at dear old England, the land of fish and chips. Now along comes curry, Indian dishes spread with cumin, coriander, and turmeric. There are more curry restaurants in London than in New Delhi or Bombay."

Virginia said, "What in the world does that have to do with us? I think you just like to show off all you know about food, and by the looks of it, you have spent a lifetime either talking about food or eating it."

"That is not a very nice thing to say about Mr. Bush," said Rita, coming to his defense, not that he needed help.

L.T. continued on curry. "Curry, to me, is a mild stimulant. Believe me, Mr. Erickson, some curry has more punch than your Louis XIII."

E.E. rose to his feet like a pheasant shot out of the bushes, "Stop all this nonsense. Let us get on with my objective: find the killer of my Arboretum rose bushes."

Moore rose to his feet also, "Please continue, Madeline, with your findings."

Madeline, for the second time, hit the crystal glass with a fork. "We have had enough talk about food and curry. Let us get back to roses and Rosenkraatz."

"Please do," agreed Virginia.

Madeline said, "Let me get to Mr. L.T. Bush, who thinks he knows who killed the roses and why. Before he says anything more, I tell you he is wrong!"

With that accusation, L.T. rose to his feet, a little unsteadily, after three Louis XIII's. "Listen, little girl," he said, "take the blindfold off your lovely eyes."

Rita Rosetta didn't like the way things were going, so she said, "What a wonderful club. And such a lovely centerpiece, isn't it?" With this observation, she looked to Virginia for help in changing the conversation.

Virginia helped her by stating, "Mr. Erickson wouldn't belong to anything but the best."

"That is right, Virginia," chimed in John Jones.

L.T. Bush didn't like the change in topic. "That is enough of this mutual admiration society. Now on with the rose killers."

Suddenly up jumped Wendall Holmes and addressed L.T. Bush. "Are you prepared to back up with facts what you are about to say?"

"My statements are purely conjectural," L.T. replied.

Rita Rosetta said, "Thank you, Virginia, for your agreeing with me about what a wonderful club this is. And how great Mr. Erickson is to bring us here."

Bernard Crow had not been heard from since the meal began, but now he stood up in what appeared to be protest about what was going on. "While all this commotion was going on, Amy stooped over John Jones' shoulder and whispered in his ear. Care to tell us, Amy, what you wanted to know?"

"Just that a member of the golf committee wanted to know who saw Jones get that hole in one on the thirteenth tee this year," Amy said.

"Why do they want to know that?" Jones asked. "Don't they believe it. The pro even said I did it."

"They don't believe everything the pro tells them," Amy responded.

"Who is out there in the hall asking these questions?" Jones wanted to know.

"Leonard Lee, the contractor, and Clem Masons, the psychiatrist," said Amy.

"You tell them that my boss, E.E. Erickson, was with me when I got that hole-in-one. Ask him for verification if they want to know," Jones responded, now getting irritated.

Amy said, "I think they believe you, so they are going to make a granite memorial with your name on it and post it by the hole."

"Is that granite going to look like a cemetery marker? If so, I don't want to be buried out there," replied John.

"I'll tell them everything you said," Amy said and then walked out the door.

Bernard Crow waited impatiently until Amy left, then he turned to Captain Moore. "Captain Moore, would you tell us about this letter to Rosenkraatz?"

Moore rose slowly. "Certainly. Mr. Crow was in possession of a letter addressed to Mr. Rosenkraatz that the deceased had given him before the lecture. The paramedics then handed him a second letter. The latter letter is a hex which mentions the poem 'Sister Helen,' which the good librarian who works with Bebe Daniels said Holmes inquired about on one of his trips to the library." At this point, Moore turned to Holmes and asked, "Did you write that letter, Mr. Holmes?"

Holmes, taken aback, said, "Yes, I did write that letter, but only in jest. I had no intention of saying that Rosenkraatz had little time to live once a certain candle, a figure of him, burned out. To me it was just a joke."

"Some joke," Crow said.

"No one was more surprised than I when Rosenkraatz turned up dead," explained Holmes.

Madeline then asked, "As a member of the distinguished Sherlock Holmes Society, you must have your deductions on the perpetrator of this heinous crime?"

"All I can deduce is that it had to be someone in this room tonight," Holmes answered.

"Why do you say that?" asked Moore.

"Look around you, Mr. Detective," replied Holmes. "Do you see a killer in this nice, friendly atmosphere?"

All this time E.E. was fascinated by the conversation and couldn't help but butt in, "Don't look at me!"

"This is no laughing matter, Mr. Erickson," said Madeline.

Moore stopped his daughter from saying any more. "What motive would any person have to kill this gentle rose lover?"

Holmes couldn't be stopped from answering: "Sex, money, revenge."

"When did you become such an expert on murders, Mr. Holmes?" asked Madeline?

E.E. couldn't remain silent any longer as he snarled, "Again, I want us to get back to my business at the Arboretum."

Holmes paid no attention to E.E.'s plea for more information on who killed his rose bushes. "You are no doubt familiar with the old poem: 'Lizzie Borden took an axe / gave her mother forty whacks. / When she saw what she had done, / gave her father forty-one'? From my investigation of the Lizzie Borden case, I told the members of our Sherlock Society that Lizzie Borden went free because the prosecution in the case had not proved that she had the way, the means and, most importantly, the opportunity to kill her father and her stepmother."

Moore rose to his feet to ask Holmes: "Why do you know so much about this oddball case of murder?"

Holmes replied, "As a member of the Sherlock Holmes Society, we make it a point to analyze all crimes with world-wide publicity."

"May I ask you a question, Mr. Holmes?" Madeline asked.

"Please do Miss Madeline."

"You said the letter you sent to Mr. Rosenkraatz about the Sister Helen poem was sent in jest."

"Yes," said Holmes.

"He jests at scars who never felt a wound," quoted Moore.

"Please, Father," said Madeline, "we don't need Shakespeare, even though he has said many things about murder in his many plays."

"You're right, of course," said Moore, who turned to E.E. and asked, "How long have you known Rita Rosetta?"

"The floral girl?"

"To be frank with you, the former nun who, as I understand it, furnishes you and your secretary with roses every week."

E.E. replied, "I have known Rita since grade school at Como Park Elementary school, a long time ago."

"Do you remember anything particular about her?"

"I was surprised when she became a nun."

"Why?"

"She was a tomboy; she played with the boys in all the sports of the time."

"Such as?"

"Baseball and football."

"That is no longer unusual," said Madeline.

Moore continued, "So you were surprised when she became a nun?"

"Stunned is the word," replied E.E.

"Why?" questioned Moore.

"She wanted to be the quarterback in the Little League in Como Park. In baseball she always wanted to be the pitcher. She just wanted to lead, not follow."

At the same time while E.E. was talking about Rita, he got up from his plush chair and closed the drapes so no one out on the putting green of the golf course could spy, even though it was dark.

"Is there anything else you know about Rita that you can tell us?" inquired Madeline.

"You must know she gives me roses every week for my office."

"Yes, we have heard that."

"Not only that, but she has come up with a new hybrid rose that is sensationally beautiful. In fact, it has been put in my rose collection at the Arboretum for exhibition. It was there until some nut destroyed the bushes during Ralph Rosenkraatz's slide showing."

"You mean the night before the slide show," said Moore.

"Whatever," said an exasperated Erickson.

"Why is that rose so special?" asked Moore. "All the roses I have seen look alike to me even though the colors may have been different."

"This rose is a special white and crimson, with the white part in the middle and a crimson-like bouquet on the outer rim. It must have been destroyed by whoever vandalized my plot in the Arboretum," moaned E.E.

"I sure wish I had been able to see it," Madeline said.

"So do I," Moore added.

All this attention was making Rita uncomfortable, and she wiggled in her chair. Bush had finally succumbed to the alcohol and sat in a daze. Virginia and Jones whispered to each other occasionally. Holmes' and Crows' eyes were riveted on the threesome at the head of the table.

"What more can you tell us about this unusual rose of Rita's?" asked Madeline.

"I'll tell you," said E.E. "Crow asked me to help Rita sell it to one of the big wholesale florists."

"Did you help?" inquired Moore.

"I'll say I helped. I sent it to my hotel in Portland, the 'City of Roses,' and soon the big florists were jumping at a chance to learn the secrets of the hybrid. The understanding was that Rita would get a commission on each license sold."

"Needless to say, Rita was ecstatic?" Madeline asked.

Erickson nodded. "But there was one thing that Rita didn't like."

"And what was that?" Madeline questioned.

"Bernard Crow told Ralph Rosenkraatz all about the Rita Rose. She didn't like that."

"Why?"

"She felt that a well-known figure in the rose world like Rosenkraatz could find a way to steal the credit for her find."

"Did she know Rosenkraatz?" Moore asked.

E.E. answered, "She knew only about Rosenkraatz and what he did to Crow's sister."

"She didn't like Rosenkraatz, but she didn't even know him?" Madeline asked in disbelief.

"You got that right, Miss Madeline," E.E. replied. "But she knew him by reputation. Everyone did."

"Where did Rita develop this rose?" asked Moore.

"At her shop," E.E. answered, "but I coaxed her to display it in my plot at the Arboretum."

"And she agreed?" asked Madeline.

"Why not? It didn't cost her a dime!"

"Was this Rita Rose bush in your plot in the Arboretum when someone destroyed the bushes the day of the Rosenkraatz slide showing?" asked Madeline.

"Yes."

"Well," concluded Madeline, "we can eliminate Rita from destroying her own exclusive rose, can't we?" At that point, Madeline smiled at Rita, who blushed.

"I don't know about that," E.E. said. "She might have feared that Rosenkraatz might steal the rose and claim it was his discovery."

Amy, who had entered the room to clear some of the dishes, said to Erickson, "The big fat man wants another Louis XIII."

"Go ahead, but no more. How many has he had already?" asked Erickson.

"Four."

"Keep an eye on him," said Erickson to Madeline. "We don't want any violence here at the club."

"I certainly will," said Madeline as Amy left to get another drink.

"Where did the Arboretum find this big lug, anyway? In the Como Tavern?" E.E. asked.

Moore grinned and said, "The Arboretum didn't find him; he found the Arboretum." After a brief laugh, Moore said, "I think we need to question Crow. You know the old saying don't you, E.E., 'The guilty flee when no man pursueth'?"

"Just how does that fit into this picture, Father?" asked Madeline.

"It doesn't, but I always like to quote it," Moore replied.

Everyone was having a wonderful time. L.T. Bush was finishing his rendition of the ballad "The Shooting of Dan McGrew."

"I suppose you can thank Louis XIII for that," said E.E.

Moore couldn't help himself by adding: "A bunch of the boys were whooping it up in the Old Malamute saloon."

"Father!" cried Madeline, "there is no need for your adding to the entertainment. We have more serious things to attend to, right Mr. Erickson?"

"Right, Madeline."

Madeline turned to Crow. Like the others in the room, he was ignoring the three people at the head of the table and was having his own conversation. "We'd like to ask you a few questions," she said.

"Why?" questioned Crow.

"Primarily, Mr. Crow," offered Madeline, "because

no one better than you can help us find out who killed Mr. Erickson's plot of roses in the Arboretum."

"Any ideas, Crow?" asked Moore, getting down to business after his daughter's scolding.

"I have a terrible admission to make, Mr. Erickson," said a sheepish Crow.

"Go ahead," said Erickson. "What is it?"

"Before I make this confession, I want you to promise not to get violent," requested Crow.

"Why would I possibly get violent with you, my friend?" asked Erickson.

"You said at one time that you would kill the person who killed your Arboretum rose bushes, right?"

"That's right," replied Erickson, "but I don't know if kill is the right word. But whoever did it would get some action from me for all the time and money I have spent over there in your Arboretum."

Bernard Crow settled back in his chair and began a long, sad story of the burnt bushes.

"I will explain to Detectives Michael and Madeline Moore the background of the destruction of the roses. Then, when you hear the whole story, Mr. Erickson, you will understand. As you have already stated, Rita Rosetta, who furnishes you with a steady supply of roses from her floral shop, discovered what she, E.E., and I thought was an amazing new hybrid rose. I persuaded Mr. Erickson to market it in his hotels, which he agreed to do, with Rita getting a good hefty commission. He even went to the bother of sending the roses to his hotel in Portland, the city of roses, to get the city's help. Needless to say, the rose was a sensation in Portland. Rita started to make money. Our so-called friend Ralph Rosenkraatz heard about this rose and wanted to get it for himself. You must realize the original hybrid was growing right in the middle of E.E.'s plot at the Arboretum."

"Just a minute," interrupted E.E., "with the income from this rose she could retire from the floral shop in five years. That is how good it is. Why did you think this rose should have been destroyed?"

Crow nodded, then continued in a low voice so no one else in the room could hear, "You're right, but I made the mistake of telling Rosenkraatz all about the new rose and where he could see it. Although I knew about Rosenkraatz's reputation for stealing hybrids, I was so excited I couldn't help myself. When I found out he had been trying to get some shoots from the plants, I was scared that he would take credit for the new rose. Rather than jeopardize the whole deal for Rita, I decided the night before the slide showing to destroy the bushes, not realizing I would wreck the whole area of roses."

"How did you go about killing these rose bushes the night before the meeting?" asked Madeline.

"I got a can of Roundup. I didn't know at the time that it would be a week to ten days before it was totally effective. So on the morning of the showing, much to my surprise, the roses still looked pretty good. So I got a can of gasoline and threw it over the whole area and that did the trick."

"So this is the end of the mystery?" E.E. asked rhetorically. "Crow, what are you going to do about replacing my roses?"

"I shall have your plot replaced at once, Mr. Erickson," assured Crow.

"As far as I am concerned," E.E. announced, "this party is over. I found out what I wanted to know. I knew from the beginning that my secretary never thought of wrecking my plot at the Arboretum."

Much to E.E.'s surprise, Captain Moore had a few things to say before Erickson broke the gathering broke up.

"This is your party, Mr. Erickson, and you can stop it anytime you want. But before you do, my daughter and I would like to thank you for the most unusual invitation. It gave us both a chance to observe the suspects more."

"Did it give you any leads to the murder of Rosenkraatz?" asked E.E.

Madeline jumped in to say the murder case was far from closed.

"I don't consider myself an expert on crime and crime detection," said Erickson in an immodest manner, "but I think if you consider who out there had the means, the opportunity, and the motive, you'll find your killer."

"That is true, Mr. Erickson," said Madeline, but before he could stop beaming, she added, "so what do you have to say about the fact that the poisoned peanut butter sandwich came from one of your hotel's catering services?"

"Who told you that?" said a red-faced Erickson.

"I can't divulge my sources just yet," replied Madeline, "but you still haven't answered my question."

"I'm sure you would understand why I did not want the word to get out that the poison sandwich came from my hotel catering service," Erickson stammered.

"He was the only volunteer to order a peanut butter sandwich, right Captain Moore?" asked Crow.

"That's right, so it makes it look as if someone in the hotel catering service must have been told to poison the peanut butter sandwich," replied Moore.

"Nobody in my hotel had anything to do with this!" Erickson insisted. "You can't prove it."

"We aren't deliberately out to get anyone, Mr. Erickson," Moore assured him. "We just want to solve a murder. I know what bad publicity can come from word going around that your catering service poisoned somebody."

"I am not wasting any more of my time. I have found out what I wanted to know," said Erickson testily.

"Fine, if that's the way you want it," said Madeline, "but if we don't get some more information tonight, then we'll have to work under the assumption that someone in your organization did the killing, and that will be in all the newspapers tomorrow."

Erickson was silent for a while and weighed his

options. None of them appeared good, but he figured he might as well put up with a few more minutes of pointless interrogation rather than thousands of hours of public relations work to repair a bad reputation.

"I hardly think anyone who is a murderer will confess as Crow did," said Erickson, "but if you think it will help."

E.E. went to the door and called for the Amy. In a few seconds, Amy appeared at the door, "Yes, sir?"

"Make sure all the guests get whatever they want to drink. I want to make sure they are all having a good time," Erickson ordered.

"I'm sure they're having a good time," said Amy. "Mr. Bush is just about through reciting 'The Midnight Ride of Paul Revere.'"

The two detectives, Erickson and Crow had been so immersed in Crow's story that they failed to notice the party going on around them.

E.E., Moore, Madeline, and Crow stood up and to the surprise of all the volunteers, E.E. stepped forward and made this statement: "We have found the culprit who did away with my rose bushes at the Arboretum. There he is," Erickson said pointing to the curator, "Bernard Crow. He had good reasons which I will not go into at this time, but you are all off the hook as suspects in the killing of the bushes."

Holmes was disappointed that he had missed solving the crime against the roses. "How are you two doing with the solution of the killing of Rosenkraatz?" he asked Moore and Madeline.

"Why is this of concern to you, Mr. Holmes?" asked Madeline.

"My Sherlock Holmes society is anxiously awaiting the outcome of this unsolved crime," he replied.

Amy brought another round of drinks, but announced that the Louis XIII was all gone.

"Who in the hell has been drinking it?" demanded Erickson.

"Mr. Bush and Ms. Rosetta," Amy said. "You gave me permission to serve them."

"I'll own the bar if you keep giving that expensive stuff away," complained E.E.

"Mr. Erickson, may I try to help out at your hotels?" asked Madeline.

"Certainly," replied an exasperated Erickson.

"If, as you claim, your hotel's peanut butter sandwich didn't do Rosenkraatz in, what else did you have at the lunch break?" Madeline asked.

Bush, who had started listening, jumped in. "I'll tell you what else we had."

"Yes?" asked Madeline.

"We all had Coke at the time we ate our sandwiches," Bush said, slurring his words.

"Was it right out of the can?" asked Madeline.

"Now that I think about it, no," volunteered Bebe Daniels.

"Are you saying that someone got ice and distributed the Coke in glasses?" asked Madeline.

"You're right, by god," said a now interested Erickson. "That is precisely how we got it."

Moore observed, "Then someone could have poisoned the glass of Coke served to Rosenkraatz?"

"I think that's a ridiculous conclusion," said Holmes

"If you can spare a minute before everybody goes home, I would like to ask each volunteer a question," Moore asked E.E.

"O.K., but hurry it up."

To L.T., Moore asked, "Who gave you the Coke?"

"My little old buddy here, Rita."

To Bebe Daniels, he asked, "Who gave you the Coke?"

"Rita Rosetta."

To Crow, he asked the same question, and his answer was the same as the rest, "The Coke from Rita!"

To Virginia, he asked, "Where did you get the Coke?"

"Sweet little Rita gave me mine," said a sarcastic Virginia.

"And of course we can't ask Rosenkraatz, but we must believe that he got his from Rita, too," said Captain Moore.

With this final statement, Rita stood up from her chair and fainted. Madeline dashed to her side. "Give her some air," she cried.

"Make sure it isn't loaded with Coke," laughed a hard-hearted Erickson.

"Some things we don't know yet. Let's not be too quick to accuse the Rita. We still don't know if there was poison in the Coke," said Moore.

Meanwhile, Rita was slowly regaining consciousness. She gasped, "I did give Mr. Rosenkraatz a Coke, but it was given to me by Mr. Holmes."

Holmes rose quickly. "I did not tell her to give the Coke to Rosenkraatz; she's drunk from the Louis XIII!" He was almost hysterical.

"It seem this is much ado about nothing," said an observant Virginia. "We don't even know if the Coke was poisoned, do we Detective Moore?"

"No we don't, not yet. But we will find out," promised Moore.

"But if it were poisoned, I surly wouldn't sleep well tonight if I were Holmes," said L.T. Bush.

"This is no time for speculation," said E.E., "but I do agree with you, Mr. Bush."

Then Rita cried out for all to hear, "I didn't know the Coke was poisoned. If it was, all I know is Mr. Holmes told me to be sure that Rosenkraatz got the Coke he gave me."

"This little girl has had too much of Louis XIII!" Holmes shouted again.

Realizing that nothing more could be done, the Moores told the volunteers they could leave, but not to go too far. With that, the Ritz party ended.

# Chapter Ten

A couple days passed. Moore met Madeline for lunch at the Green Mill. As he spooned the soup of the day, he began the conversation "So the coroner said there was no way of knowing whether Rosenkraatz was poisoned with a sandwich or a Coke. There could have been backwash from the sandwich in what was left of the Coke or some of the Coke left on the sandwich, but someone had picked up the glasses during the time the paramedics worked on Rosenkraatz, so that evidence has disappeared."

"So just because Rosenkraatz had his own sandwich didn't mean it was full of poison?"

"Right, Madeline. And another thing, they pinpointed the poison a little better.

"And the conclusion?"

"Rodenticides," said Moore.

"You mean rat poison?"

"Precisely," said Moore not even taking a breath to get some more soup into his mouth. "Also under this category come cyanides and pesticides."

"That's interesting," said Madeline, "because I've been doing a little research on an interesting poison listed under hydrocyanic acid."

"And that was?"

"Prussic acid," Madeline answered.

"Why is Prussic acid so interesting to you, Madeline?"

"After Rita Rosetta said that Holmes gave her the drink to give Rosenkraatz, I looked into more information on Holmes."

"And what did you discover?" Moore asked.

"First of all, I looked up the address of the Sherlock Holmes Society. I talked to Joe Miller, who happens to be secretary and president of the club."

"Go on," said Moore.

"Miller said he knew Wendall Holmes very well, and was most impressed on Holmes' knowledge of the world-famous trial of Lizzie Borden. Holmes was convinced she did it, according to Miller. Holmes told Miller there wasn't a doubt in his mind."

"What does that have to do with Prussic acid?" asked Moore.

"I'm getting to that, but first let me tell you more about the secretary of the Holmes Society.

"Why?" asked Moore.

"For one thing, all that humming he was always doing, even during their meetings at the Club."

"Humming doesn't make him nuts or a murderer," observed Moore. "What else did you find out?"

"You're right," said Madeline, "but I also discovered he had spent a short period of time in the St. Peter Asylum for the insane."

"How long was he there?"

"Only a few years," answered Madeline. "A bevy of psychiatrists agreed he was harmless. Now he works as a candy jobber and letter carrier."

"He sells candy?"

"That's right," responded Madeline. "He sells candy mainly to wholesalers, who in turn sell it to supermarkets."

"Why was he put in St. Peter?" asked Moore, getting more interested.

"He is what a psychiatrist would call schizophrenic."

"So he must be on some kind of medication," Moore said.

"Sure," said Madeline, "but sometimes people forget to take their medications, and then. . . ." She shrugged her soldiers.

"They can get delusional," offered Moore.

"That's right."

"I'm still trying to see how the demise of Rosenkraatz fits in here," said Moore

"In my own research of the Lizzie Borden case, I found a note to the effect that on the day before this mayhem, Lizzie Borden had gone to a chemist's shop, what we now know as a drug store, to buy some Prussic acid. She didn't tell the druggist why she wanted it. Holmes told the secretary of the society that she obviously wanted it to poison her stepmother, someone Lizzie did not like."

"So Lizzie planned to get rid of her stepmother with a little poison," Moore interrupted.

"Right," said Madeline.

"And Holmes wanted to commit a copycat crime?" asked Moore.

"Could be," Madeline said. "He may not have been thinking clearly, particularly since Lizzie received a half million dollars from the estate and it doesn't appear that Holmes had any reason other than a historical interest in the Borden case."

"Your tale fascinates me," said Moore, "but it seems a bit far fetched. Plus, you have no proof that the drink carried the poison and not the peanut butter sandwich."

Just then, someone humming "When Irish Eyes are Smiling" came into the room with Rita Rosetta.

"Speak of the devil," said Moore. "What in the world are they doing here?"

"Why don't you go and ask them?" Madeline suggested.

"I'll go along with that idea," said Moore. "Just let me finish my soup."

The hostess put Holmes and Rosetta in a both next

to the two detectives, then someone came to take their drink orders, and left.

Before Moore got to the bottom of his bowl, however, the server returned for Holmes' and Rosetta's orders.

"What do you recommend?" asked Holmes of the server.

"We're known for our award winning pizza," said the server.

"Sounds good," said Holmes. "And for you, Rita?"

"I'll have the same."

Moore was just getting up and Holmes said to Rita, "While we wait, let's get this confession over with. Your detectives are right in the booth next to us as the sergeant at the police station said they would be."

"I know," said a suddenly sobbing Rita.

Without wasting a moment, Holmes stepped over to the booth where Moore and Madeline sat. "You and I have met, right detectives? You remember Rita Rosetta?"

"Right," Moore answered.

"Right," Madeline repeated. "We were all together at Mr. Erickson's big fete."

"Why all this formality, Mr. Holmes?" asked Moore. "We all have met before."

"I want to bring you up-to-date on what has happened between Rita and me since the Ritz party. This poor little girl has fallen in love with me, and I with her," boasted Holmes.

"I don't know what came over me," cried Rita. "He took me home after the Ritz banquet and since then we have hardly been apart."

Madeline looked in wonder at this couple: Rita, the floral shop owner, and Holmes, the former inmate at St. Peter's asylum. Madeline thought, but did not say, love indeed is blind."

"Rita urged me to come clean about the demise of Rosenkraatz," Holmes said sadly.

"Come clean?" Moore inquired.

"Tell all," sobbed Rita, who just couldn't stop crying.

"Tell us all about what, Mr. Holmes?" Madeline asked.

Moore turned to Madeline and said, "Get out your notebook and take this all down for the record."

Madeline immediately dug into her purse and pulled out a notebook. Before she did, she gave Holmes his Miranda warning, but he waved that aside. "I know what I'm doing."

"Now, Wendall," advised Rita, "tell Mr. Moore and Madeline exactly what you told me about what happened to Mr. Rosenkraatz."

So Wendall began his story: "You are aware of the message I admitted sending Rosenkraatz on the day he started his slide showing? You know all about Sister Helen and the burning of his wax image? I won't go into that, but you know the outcome: when the wax figure melted to nothing, Rosenkraatz would be dead!"

"I recall reading the letter," admitted Moore.

"All the time I was in the asylum, I had chances to read mystery stories by the hundreds and became quite interested in them. In a devious manner, I soon realized the foolproof murder would be to kill someone with no apparent motive, skipping all this nonsense about greed, lust, and power!" Holmes said.

"Go on," urged Rita.

"When I was released from the asylum, I told the psychiatrists I was harmless. I immediately sought out and found the Sherlock Holmes Society, where everyone is interested in murder cases. Sister Helen's approach fascinated me, and I became a volunteer for the Arboretum as a hobby, not for any love of roses. When I heard that the great authority on roses, Ralph Rosenkraatz, would give a lecture and a slide showing on the who, what, and where of roses, I decided to go. Then I thought of the Sister Helen idea, since this guy meant nothing to me. But, I thought I could put a scare in him with this wax image gag, and sent the letter, as I have said before, in jest."

Holmes continued, "But when he didn't cancel the lecture, I was insulted. Because he was the only one who got a peanut butter sandwich, you experts thought it was the poison in the sandwich. No way. It was in the Coke I gave Rita to give Rosenkraatz while he was having his lunch."

Rita now stopped sobbing. Holmes was doing what she wanted him to do: confess all the morbid details of Rosenkraatz's death.

"Madness will not be my plea, but sanity. I knew what I was doing all the time. If caught, which I never was, I didn't want to go back to the asylum with all the nuts. I would rather go to jail and eventually, on good behavior, get out and then happily marry Rita, which she has promised to do, even though the wait may be a couple of years."

"I will wait for you forever, Wendall," Rita promised, now smiling cheerfully.

Just then, the waitress arrived with the pizza.

"I have this last request," pleaded Holmes. "Let me finish this meal before you take me in."

"Your wish is granted," promised Moore. He turned to the waitress and ordered another bowl of soup.

"What are we going to do to celebrate the closing of this case?" asked Madeline.

Moore looked at his watch. "It's Tuesday. I say we go to Mitch's Cocktail Lounge for some Mulligan Stew tonight."